The MAGN

LIZZIE BROWN

and the

Devil's Hound

Books in

THE MAGNIFICENT LIZZIE BROWN

series

THE MYSTERIOUS PHANTOM

THE DEVIL'S HOUND

THE GHOST SHIP

THE FAIRY CHILD

The Magnificent Lizzie Brown and the Devil's Hound

VICKI LOCKWOOD

Curious Fox

With special thanks to Adrian Bott

First published in 2015 by Curious Fox,
an imprint of Capstone Global Library Limited,
7 Pilgrim Street, London, EC4V 6LB
Registered company number: 6695582

www.curious-fox.com

Series created by Hothouse Fiction
www.hothousefiction.com

Cover design by Steve Mead
Illustrations by Eva Morales

ISBN 978 1 78202 065 3

19 18 17 16 15
1 3 5 7 9 10 8 6 4 2

A CIP catalogue for this book is available from the British Library.

Typeset in Adobe Garamond Pro by Hothouse Fiction Ltd

Printed and bound by CPI Group (UK) Ltd, Croydon, CRO 4YY

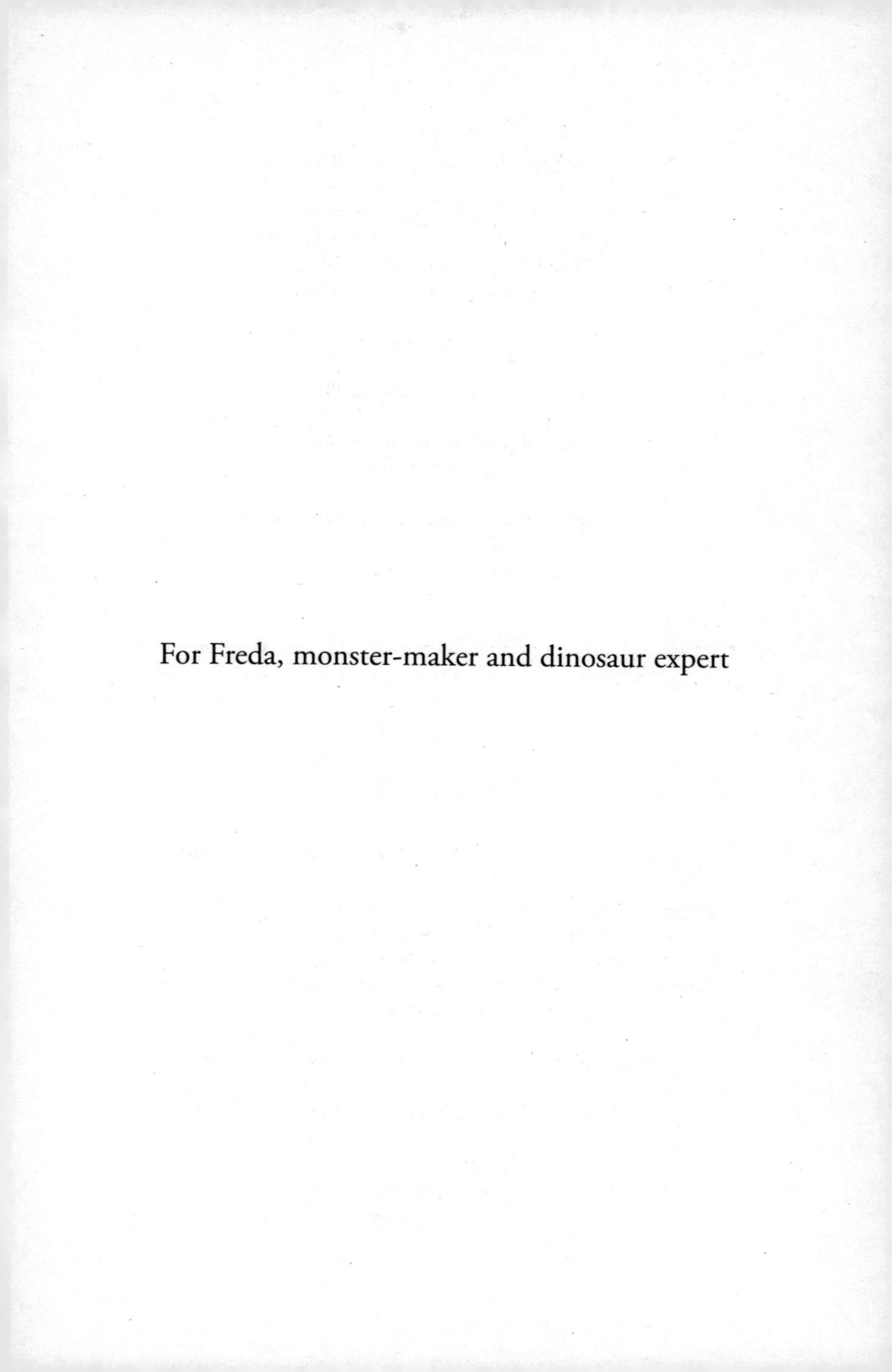

For Freda, monster-maker and dinosaur expert

CHAPTER 1

'Two hundred and seventeen,' said Lizzie Brown, sighing loudly.

The cow she had just counted looked up at her through the pouring rain and chewed thoughtfully. The bright gold paint on the side of Lizzie's circus wagon declared her to be 'THE MAGNIFICENT LIZZIE BROWN, Mystic Wonder of our Age!' and 'Unmasker of the Notorious London Phantom!' Rain hammered it now as if the heavens were trying to wash away all traces of her former glory.

Right now, Lizzie felt about as magnificent as a soggy sock. Circus life was so intense and exciting when the shows were on that you somehow forgot all the travelling you had to do. It was like falling from a brightly coloured trapeze into a tub of cold, grey porridge.

Nora and Erin, the Incredible Sullivan Twins, were taking it in turns to hold the reins. Their red hair stood out brightly next to Lizzie's own chestnut-brown locks. The horses pulling the wagon were a temperamental new pair, who would be performing with the twins, so the girls were doing their own driving for a change. They softly sang Irish folk songs together to the rhythm of the jolting caravan. Lizzie didn't know the tunes, so she'd decided to count cows.

'What in the world are you doing that for?' Erin asked.

'It passes the time,' said Lizzie with a shrug.

And what a lot of time there was to pass. Fitzy's Travelling Circus had been plodding its way through mile after mile of North London countryside for hours now. Lizzie was sick and tired of quaint stone bridges, sullen young men on haycarts and groups outside village pubs staring at the circus as it went past. *Good manners don't cost anything*, her ma had always said.

A shout came from the head of the convoy:

'Kensal Green up ahead!'

Thank goodness, Lizzie thought. *That's our pitch. We can stop soon.*

Although this was the first time the circus had returned to London since Lizzie had joined a month ago, it didn't feel like coming home. Most likely it never would.

London held too many ghosts for Lizzie. Memories of her father's fists, of hunger and begging on the streets, came back to her. Her pa had nearly broken her arms more than once. Sooner or later, in one of his dreadful drunken rages, he'd have broken her neck. That was the way stories like Lizzie's ended in the London slums. Fitzy had saved her from all that, and she'd never forget her debt to him.

The circus had brought her happiness like she'd never known, filling her heart as well as her belly. Compared to the horrors of violence and slow starvation, this endless rain was a small price to pay, especially as she had friends like Nora and Erin to huddle up to. The long journeys might be dull sometimes, but she'd never go back to the life she'd had before.

She'd run away from Rat's Castle, the slum where she'd grown up, only to find a new home among the colourful strangers of Fitzy's Travelling Circus. Fitzy had taken her on as a fortune-teller's assistant, only to discover that he had a *genuine* fortune-teller on his hands.

When her strange powers had first shown themselves, Lizzie had been more surprised than anyone. All that supernatural mystic-shmystic nonsense turning out to be true? It didn't sit right with her, but she couldn't deny it.

All her life she'd had vivid dreams that often came true, but she'd always dismissed it as coincidence. Ironically, it was while the old fortune-teller, Madame Aurora, had been teaching her how to *fake* a reading that her powers had come to the fore. Nowadays, she could see people's futures just by looking into their palms.

Her gift was her living now that she worked at Fitzy's. People paid well for a reading from the Magnificent Lizzie Brown. The sign on her trailer was no idle boast, either. She really had revealed the true identity of the fearsome Phantom, the masked burglar who had terrorized London. It had been the first – and so far only – victory for Lizzie and her crew of crime-fighting circus friends, the Penny Gaff Gang.

'Easy, Victoria!' Nora said, as one of the beautiful black horses pulling their trailer whinnied and tossed her head. 'It's only a cow.'

'What's Kensal Green like, Lizzie?' Erin asked.

'Never been,' Lizzie said. 'Heard there's not much there, though. Railway, canal, a few streets of houses.'

'So long as there's punters to put on a show for, that's what matters,' Nora said.

Lizzie peered ahead, to where dim shapes were coming into view through the misty rainfall. 'Are we at the site yet?'

'We must be!' Erin said.

There was a row of trees just off the road, and as they drew closer Lizzie saw it was the fringe of an enormous park. White stone buildings showed through the trees. The rain brought out the sad, sweet smell of cypresses.

Nora whistled. 'That's a belter of a pitch. Look at all the lawns! Smooth and flat as a billiard table, so they are.'

'Must be a park for proper toffs,' agreed Erin. 'Fitzy knows what he's about. You two beauties will be paid for in no time, won't you now?' She was talking to Albert and Victoria, the two night-black stunners who were pulling the caravan. Lizzie had never seen more beautiful horses in her life. Fitzy hadn't been able to resist them and had bought them on credit, risking a huge amount of money.

'Come on, Fitzy,' Erin said, frowning. 'Why aren't we heading off the road?'

'Because that ain't our site,' Lizzie said.

'Sure it's not? And how would you know?'

'Because,' Lizzie said with grim satisfaction, 'it ain't the sort of place for a circus to set up. It ain't even a park.'

'So what in the world is it if it's not a park, I'd like to know?'

Before Lizzie could answer, a set of gates came into view. With a silver sound of jingling harnesses and a clop of hooves on stone, a strange procession emerged from the rain and began to pass through the park gates. A gentleman wearing black and carrying an ebony cane walked in front, with a slow measured tread and downcast eyes.

Two gigantic black horses followed, decked out in livery that was as black as their coats. Tall feathery plumes rose from their heads like jets of ink. They were pulling a long, flat carriage that was overflowing with white lilies, startlingly bright against all the black.

In amongst the soaking flowers lay a long, dark casket. Erin and Nora instantly crossed themselves, superstitiously warding off evil in the presence of a dead person. Lizzie might once have smiled at that, but not nowadays.

'It's not a park, it's a cemetery!' Erin exclaimed.

'Kensal Green Cemetery,' said Lizzie, feeling uneasy and proud at the same time. 'Them white buildings are tombs. Goes on for flippin' miles.'

'I've heard about it,' Nora said with a shudder.

'Everybody has,' Erin added. 'The stories they tell… Oh, I hope we're not setting up anywhere near. Me skin's crawling just looking at it.'

The funeral procession went on and on. A host of mourners, women in veils and gentlemen in top hats, passed by with their heads bowed. Many of the women were weeping, swabbing at their eyes with black silk handkerchiefs. The circus people at the front removed their hats respectfully as they passed.

Angry glares were the response. The mourners didn't want to see jolly circus caravans going past. Lizzie heard some of them grumbling: 'Couldn't they have taken a different road?' and, 'How could they? A *circus*? The vulgarity of it!' One woman fainted dramatically and had to be revived with smelling salts. Lizzie felt awkward and shifted uncomfortably.

'There's no call for that,' Nora said. 'Sure it wasn't our fault that we were on the road at the same time as them.'

'Toffs,' Erin snorted, as if that explained everything. 'Think how much that funeral there must have cost! Everything tricked out in black, silks and satins if you please, all for some poor soul who can't even see it!'

Lizzie felt a stab of pain right under her ribs. When her mother had died, there had been no money for a funeral. There hadn't even been a coffin. The man had come and stitched Ma up into the long white sheet. Her father had yelled at her to stop snivelling, but she'd cried anyway. Then her mother had been bundled onto a cart, driven through the streets and lowered with ropes into a hole in the ground. There were other white bundles down there, strewn with earth, and other families crying.

That was all her mother got. A pauper's grave, without even a gravestone to mark it.

The year before, her brother John had died from phosphorus poisoning. Matchstick factory workers often went that way. Lizzie had saved up a few farthings for some flowers, but her father found it and spent it on drink. John was buried the same way. Another muddy pit, and a few mumbled words from a vicar who had no idea who any of them were.

Lizzie had tried to find the graves since then, but it was hopeless. There were no grand marble monuments for the dead of the London slums. They were just thrown away like so much rubbish.

Her caravan was passing the funeral procession now. Lizzie looked straight ahead. *I won't give you lot the satisfaction of rolling your eyes at me*, she thought. *You don't know what I've been through in my life.*

Victoria whinnied and shook her head. She clattered sideways for a moment, as if a horsefly had bitten her.

'Easy, girl!' Nora said, alarmed. Many of the mourners turned to stare as she struggled to calm the mare.

The casket passed through the cemetery gates. At that exact moment, Victoria reared up. Her hooves waved in the air. Someone in the crowd gave a cry of fear.

Gasps rang out as Erin leaped from her seat onto Victoria's smooth back. Hanging on with her legs, she stroked the long mane and whispered into Victoria's ears until the horse seemed calmer.

Lizzie stole a quick glance into the cemetery and saw the casket making its way up a slope towards an open grave, where a crowd was waiting.

'Wouldn't look if I were you, Lizzie,' Nora said.

'Why not? It's only a load of toffs.'

Nora lowered her voice. 'There's something in Kensal Green Cemetery you don't want coming after you. Victoria's got wind of it.'

Lizzie laughed. 'Get away.'

'Didn't you see how spooked she was?'

'She just got worried by the big crowd, didn't she, Erin?'

Still on the horse's back, Erin didn't reply.

Nora shivered and whispered, 'They say that cemetery's haunted.'

'"They" say that about *every* cemetery,' Lizzie said scornfully.

'Not like this one. Have you not heard the rhyme?

Hide your face, my darling girl,
and run, oh run for home,
For round the stones of Kensal Green,
the Devil's Hound does roam.'

'Devil's Hound, my foot!' Lizzie scoffed. Her friends could be so superstitious sometimes. 'It was the crowd that spooked her. That's all.'

'D'you think?' Nora said. 'Well, we'd best hope Victoria doesn't panic at her next sight of a crowd. We can't have her acting up like that on opening night.'

That was a frightening thought. The new horses were a big investment and Fitzy was counting on them to take part. He'd even had new posters printed, featuring the twins balancing on Albert' and Victoria's backs. They *had* to be ready to perform.

Up ahead, the convoy was moving off the road and into a green field.

'We're here!' Lizzie said. 'About time. My bottom's gone numb.'

In only a few moments, the atmosphere changed from weary boredom to frantic hard work as Fitzy's Circus set about pitching its show tent. The rain was still coming down in torrents, threatening to turn the field into a muddy swamp. First the canvas and poles had to be unpacked, then the rigging and the stakes along with the mallets to drive them in. Meanwhile, enclosures had to be set up for the animals, who all needed to be fed and watered after their journey.

Like scenes from a mad poet's dream, camels trotted past behind bearded ladies, a boy with claw-like hands and feet tucked nails into his mouth and a hammer under his arm, a woman as fat as a hot air balloon passed wicker travelling baskets to her short, smiling husband, and acrobats stood on one another's shoulders to lift tent poles into position.

It looked like chaos, but Fitzy had it all under control. Lizzie loved to watch him at work, striding from place to place with his cane under his arm. If any job needed an extra pair of hands, he'd roll up his sleeves and help, never mind the mud and wet.

'Hari!' Lizzie called, running up to help the lean Indian boy lead one of the elephants out. 'Easy, Akula. It's me!' The elephant nuzzled her fondly under the arm, making her giggle.

Once Akula was safely set up with fresh hay and a meal, Lizzie went to see where else she could be useful. Her own fortune-telling tent didn't have to be put up until later.

The Boisset family, acrobats and high-wire walkers,

were pulling up a support pole. Lizzie ran over to give them a hand. Dru Boisset was tall for his age, and everyone agreed he was turning into a handsome young man. 'You 'ave muscles,' he said approvingly.

'Do I?' Lizzie was a little mortified at that.

The French boy laughed. 'For a girl, I mean.'

'Try bending an iron bar next,' grunted Mario the strong man, giving her a wink.

One of the clowns, JoJo, was unloading crates stuffed with juggling clubs, costumes and props. Lizzie always looked forward to helping him, since he loved to try out new routines with her. 'Chuck 'em over here!' she joked. 'I'll catch them!'

JoJo stared. There were dark bags under his eyes. 'Are you going to give us a hand or not?'

Startled, Lizzie ran to take the other end of the crate. 'I was just joking.'

Jojo sighed and rubbed his sweating forehead. 'I know. Sorry, love. I'm not myself today.'

'What's the matter?'

He blinked helplessly, as if there was something he badly needed to say, but didn't dare to. 'I'm feeling a bit poorly,' he admitted.

'You go and lie down. I'll unload the rest of this stuff.'

'You sure?'

'Of course! Go and get some rest.' She patted JoJo on the back.

But the moment she touched him, her skin prickled all over. In her mind's eye, she saw a shadow. Long, ragged arms stretched out to grasp JoJo. It wore a hood and robe, but there was nothing beneath but bare bones. *Death.* Next second, it was gone.

Lizzie gasped and pulled away.

From somewhere in the distance – possibly from Kensal Green Cemetery itself – came a long mournful howl. Lizzie's blood chilled as the sound went right through her.

It was the baying of a hound...

CHAPTER 2

It was late afternoon, but the grim skies outside made it feel like evening. At least the show tent was up now. The rain drummed on the canvas with a sound like wild horses stampeding across a plain.

'Tea break,' Erin said happily. 'Come on!'

Lizzie and the twins dashed out of the show tent, shielding their heads as best they could from the lashing rain. They ducked inside the animals' tent for a quick breather.

Immediately a snarl ripped through the air, making Lizzie jump. Leo the lion was pacing up and down, glaring and occasionally roaring. Camels fidgeted and spat.

'Blimey,' Lizzie said. 'What's got into them?'

'They're spooked,' said Nora. 'Just like Victoria was.'

'Look at the elephants!' said Erin. Mo, Myrtle and Sashi, usually calm, were stamping their feet and tossing their heads. Akula trumpeted and reared up.

Just then, Hari came in, his face grim. 'Better leave them to me,' he said. 'It's easier to calm them down if there are fewer people around.'

'What's upsetting the animals?' Lizzie asked.

Hari shook his head. 'It's been a long trip. They don't like being cooped up for hours any more than we do. And the storm's making a lot of noise.'

That wasn't the whole story, Lizzie could tell. She approached Akula, with her hand held out. 'Easy, Akula. It's only me.'

'I wouldn't go near her,' said Hari. 'I know she's your friend, but she's scared right now.'

'Scared? What of?'

Hari looked down as if he'd said too much. 'The same thing half of us are scared of, I expect. Some people are saying Fitzy's made a mistake coming here, to this pitch. They think we should move on.'

'We can't!' Erin yelled. 'We'd lose money – and Albert and Victoria aren't paid for yet!' At the shrill sound of her voice, the lion roared.

Hari quickly shooed them all out of the tent. 'Come back later, when the storm's blown over,' he suggested.

Ma Sullivan, the twins' mother, had rigged up her tea tent outside the family caravan. It was cosy inside, with the entire Sullivan family gathered around a single table and some of the other circus folk visiting for a relaxing brew. Usually, the tea tent was a jolly place, full of laughter and gossip. Fitzy would often stop by and play a round of dominoes, puffing fragrant pipe smoke into the steamy air. Today, though, the girls walked into an atmosphere of gloom.

Erik the acrobat was sitting with Bungo the roustabout. The two of them made an unlikely pair, one thin and wiry as a whippet, the other stout as a walrus. Erik looked up at Lizzie with wet pale eyes, as if he expected her to explain why this black mood was hovering over everyone.

'Blimey,' Lizzie said with a nervous laugh. 'Has someone died?'

Ma Sullivan sucked air through her teeth. 'You'd best not go making jokes about that sort o' thing, Lizzie love. Not around here.'

'Those toffs said this was no place for a circus, the

moment they saw us,' Erik said.

Erin helped herself to a huge mug of tea and one of her mother's oat flapjacks. 'The animals are all of a pother. Hari's trying to calm them down.'

'What did I tell you?' Bungo said to Erik. 'It's always the animals that know when something's up. They've got a sixth sense.'

'Victoria didn't like going past … that place,' Nora said. They all glanced in the direction of Kensal Green Cemetery.

'It's not right, so it's not.' Ma Sullivan, short and draped in a shawl, went to heat up a fresh kettle full of water on the wood burner. 'The dearly departed should have a corner of some little churchyard to call their own. That's as much as any of us need. Just a quiet wee plot with a hazel tree, perhaps, and a headstone. But that place?' She shivered, making a *brrr* sound. 'It's the *size* of it that sets your teeth on edge, I don't mind saying. Acre after acre, grave after grave! It's not right.'

'That's it, Mrs S! That's just exactly it!' Bungo slurped his tea, wetting his whiskers. 'How can the dead rest easy in such a place? It's no wonder they go roving about.'

'Roving about?' Erin echoed in horror.

'Why else would the animals be upset?' Ma Sullivan said. 'Where there's graves, there's ghosts. Erin, Nora, be sure and take your rosaries with you if you have to go off the site.'

Lizzie felt a twinge of anger at all these dark mutterings. Even though she had powers she couldn't explain, it didn't mean *everything* had to be mysterious and spooky. 'It's only a cemetery,' she said boldly.

Bungo shook his shaggy head. 'You won't catch me going in there after dark. Not for a million pounds.'

'I'd go,' said Sean, one of the Sullivan brothers.

'You would not,' said Patrick, another one. 'You'd come running out after five minutes, shoutin', "Help, help, the Cú Sídhe's chasing after me!"'

'Patrick Sullivan!' Ma shouted, slamming the kettle down hard with a bang. 'Do you want to bring bad luck down on the whole lot of us, now?'

Lizzie blinked. 'What's a … what you said?' It had sounded like 'Coo Shee'.

Ma hesitated, then beckoned Lizzie over to sit with her. She leaned in close, ready to tell something important. The other Sullivans leaned in too, so they were all huddled over their tea like a gaggle of witches meeting over a cauldron.

'Sometimes they call it the Black Dog,' Ma Sullivan whispered. 'Most folk know better than to call it by its real name, except for this eejit.' She smacked Patrick lightly on the back of the head and ignored his howl of protest. 'Sometimes it prowls around the old mounds that the fair folk left behind them—'

'Fair folk?' Lizzie interrupted in disbelief. 'You can't mean … fairies?'

'Wheesht and let me tell what I've got to tell!' snapped Ma Sullivan.

Lizzie squirmed. 'Sorry.'

'Those who've seen it say it takes the form of a hound the size of a calf, all shaggy and black, with eyes like burning coals. It lurks in graveyards, waiting for foolish souls who've gone there after dark, perhaps to take a short cut, perhaps because they were doing some stupid dare that their brother put them up to.' She glared at Sean, who pretended he didn't know she meant him.

Round the stones of Kensal Green, the Devil's Hound does roam, thought Lizzie. She was sure it was all just folklore, but she listened politely. Ma Sullivan did like to spin a yarn, especially at times like this, when the thunder and the rain outside just added to the story.

'The hound goes hunting for souls to drag down to

Hell,' Ma whispered. 'If you hear it howl, you must run for safety, into a church, or at the very least into a well-lit house.'

'Or over running water,' whispered Nora.

Ma Sullivan nodded. 'If it howls again, then run all the faster. Because it howls only three times for any one person, and if you hear the last howl before you reach a safe place, then that's the end of you.'

A crack of thunder shook the tent and a figure appeared in the doorway, silhouetted by the lightning.

Everybody gasped, as if Death had come for them. But it was only Fitzy himself, in his striking multi-coloured waistcoat, with his club-footed son Malachy close behind.

'Hope I'm not interrupting your leisure time,' Fitzy said sharply. Lizzie was taken aback by the tone of his voice. He sounded moments away from an angry outburst.

'Will you take a cup of tea, Fitz?' Ma said, suddenly all smiles.

'No time for tea,' Fitzy snapped. 'There's work to do. We still have a show to put on, unless I'm much mistaken? Erin, Nora, come with me. Let's talk rehearsals.'

He turned on his heel and walked out. Ma Sullivan watched him go, then turned to her girls. 'Well? You heard him!'

Lizzie, Nora and Erin ran out into the rain. Malachy was lagging behind his father, hobbling along on his stick. They quickly caught up.

'Dad's in a foul mood,' Malachy murmured to Lizzie, too low for Fitzy to hear.

'I noticed.'

'You don't have to be psychic to see it, do you?' Malachy winced as his good foot sank into a muddy spot of ground. 'He took a chance on this pitch and it looks like it's not going to pay off.'

'Because of the rain?'

'Well, not just the rain.' Malachy glanced at the cemetery. Lizzie braced herself for more muttering about ghosts and demons, but to her relief Malachy was just as sceptical as she was. 'You know how superstitious we circus folk can be – and there aren't many tougher crowds to play to than a field full of dead people.'

Fitzy headed into the main show tent. The sawdust ring was already in place and the clowns were busy with rehearsal. Lizzie sat down to watch.

'You're on next,' Fitzy told Erin and Nora. 'Hari's on

his way with the gee-gees.'

It was always strange to see the clowns performing without costumes or make-up. Rice Pudding Pete crossed the floor with a wibbly-wobbly walk, holding up an empty tray. Lizzie knew it would have a bowl brimful with rice pudding on the night. Most of which would go straight down his trousers.

Fitzy folded his arms and looked on approvingly. Then he frowned. 'Someone's missing. Where's JoJo?'

'Can't make rehearsal, boss,' Pete called, looking apologetic.

'That's not good enough. I need all hands. Tell him to drag his lazy backside in here!'

'He can't,' Pete said, more firmly now. 'He's sick. Barely been out of bed all day.'

Fitzy let out an explosive sigh. 'Sick, eh? That's all I ruddy need. One more blessing. Malachy, next time I suggest setting up in Kensal Green, please be so good as to kick me.'

'Will do, Pop,' Malachy said.

'Did you get those new posters put up in the town, at least?'

'I sent Dru and Collette half an hour ago with a stack a foot high.'

'Good lad.' Fitzy glanced about. 'Where in hell has Hari got to?'

Lizzie had met Dru on his way to stick up the posters, along with his snooty sister Collette. The posters were bigger than usual, with yellow, purple and red ink blazing through the rain. 'Fitzy spent a fortune on these,' Dru had said approvingly. 'And look who's at the centre!' It was Erin and Nora, the Amazing Sullivan Twins, long red hair flying like banners, performing their equestrian ballet from the backs of two beautiful black horses.

Fitzy had spent a fortune on Albert and Victoria, too. A fortune he didn't have. *No wonder he's fretting*, Lizzie thought. If the rain kept the customers away, he wouldn't just lose the profits, he'd have to surrender the horses. And without the horses the posters were useless, so he'd have wasted that money too. Everything seemed like it was hanging by a thread.

At least the Sullivan boys had their own part of the equestrian act to perform. After Erin and Nora had amazed the crowds with their horseback ballet, the boys – Conor, Patrick, Sean and Brendan – would perform their Wild West routine, firing off pistols and shooting arrows at straw dummies. Lizzie respected their talent, but everyone knew it was Nora and Erin who the crowds came to see. Clearly Fitzy knew it too.

Hari finally appeared, but when he edged around the tent flap, the horses weren't with him. Even the clowns stopped in the middle of their routine and stared.

'I'm waiting,' Fitzy told him.

'I am sorry, Fitzy,' Hari said. 'The new horses aren't ready to perform.'

'Did I or did I not say I wanted them *here*, at five on the dot?' Fitzy clenched his gloved hands around his cane as if he meant to strangle the life out of it.

'It's the storm!' Hari held up his hands, helpless to do anything. 'It's made them so skittish, and Victoria's already temperamental! We need to leave them alone for a whole day at least, so they can calm down. If they could talk, they'd thank you for it.'

Fitzy shook his head. 'I can't. The horses are on the posters. That means they have to be in the show, and the show has to be rehearsed.'

Hari threw Malachy a desperate look.

'You should do what Hari says, Pop,' Malachy said. 'He knows animals better than anyone else in this circus. You've said it yourself.'

Fitzy put his arms around Nora and Erin. 'But

Hari's not going to be the one who rides them, is he? The Amazing Sullivan Twins are. They're the most experienced riders any of us have ever seen. Don't worry. They'll be fine.' Erin and Nora looked at one another nervously. 'But it *is* late, and it *is* raining, so we'll put off rehearsal until first light tomorrow. But not a second later, understood?'

'Yes, Mr Fitzgerald,' the twins said together.

Fitzy beamed, but Hari shook his head and slipped out silently.

'What could I say?' protested Nora, as Lizzie stroked Albert's soft nose. 'I didn't want to let him down.'

It was the morning of the next day. The rain had turned from a constant downpour to a light drizzle.

Lizzie stood her ground. 'You could have said no. He can't *make* you practise.'

Erin, meanwhile, was riding Victoria around and around, balancing on tiptoes on the horse's back. The acrobats were rehearsing in the main tent, so there was nowhere else to practise but outside in the rain. Hari had come to watch and stood silently, keeping a careful eye on the horses.

'Oh, but you're a beauty, aren't you,' Nora sighed as she patted Albert's glossy flank. 'We can't have the creditors taking you back, can we?'

'They are beautiful,' Lizzie agreed. 'Like – what's the word for shadow pictures cut out of black paper? It's French. Dru said it once.'

'Silhouettes,' Nora said with a smile. She vaulted onto Albert's back and rode off to join her sister. Albert's hooves churned up wet mud, spattering the air. Lizzie glanced at the sky and wished she had the power to switch the rain off.

But it was worth getting wet to watch the Sullivans in action. Even though Lizzie had seen their act many times before, their grace took her breath away. They balanced on top of the horses like ballerinas, as if invisible wings were keeping them upright, hovering weightless as hummingbirds.

They turned somersaults mid-air and landed delicately on their hands. Lizzie stifled a gasp. She didn't want to distract them. Another flip and they were on their feet again, somehow perfectly balanced despite the horses thundering along below them.

They turned, posed, spun round, balanced first on

one leg and then on one hand. *It's going to be all right*, Lizzie thought to herself. *The moment the word gets out that these two gorgeous horses and their brilliant riders are in the show, Fitzy's going to be rolling in money!*

Now for the finale. This was the real showstopper. Each twin got ready to leap through the air, do the splits and land on the other's horse. Lizzie held her breath.

Thunder boomed, echoing across the field like cannon fire.

Victoria reared up, whinnying wildly. Erin fell from her back and landed, gasping, on the muddy ground. As Erin struggled to stand up, all Lizzie could think was: *At least the ground was soft.*

But as Victoria's hooves came down, the big black horse slipped on the mud. Suddenly she was falling, legs waving wildly in the air, her head thrashing. She rolled right on top of Erin, who didn't even have time to scream.

There was a hideous cracking sound as she vanished beneath the horse's bulk.

CHAPTER 3

'Erin!' Lizzie ran into the field. *Please don't be dead, oh God, please let her be all right!* she thought wildly.

Hari sprinted in after her. Victoria was still floundering on the muddy ground, kicking her legs in a mad panic. The moment the horse saw the boy, she seemed to calm down. Hari took her reins and coaxed her gently back onto her feet.

Erin lay on her back in the mud, terribly pale. Her clothes were filthy and rain was falling in her face. Lizzie expected to see blood streaming from a wound, but there wasn't any – not yet.

Nora rode up beside them, on the verge of tears, and

quickly dismounted. 'Is she breathing?'

'I think so,' Lizzie said.

Erin let out a long moan that rose to a sob. 'It hurts!'

She's alive! No time to celebrate now. Lizzie tried to help her up. 'What hurts? Where did she get you?'

Erin put one arm around Lizzie and managed to stand up.

'She landed on my wrist.' Erin held her arm in front of them. It looked red and swollen. Her lips were trembling.

'Let me see,' said Hari. 'Mmm. It's taken a nasty knock. You'd better go and see Fitzy.'

'It's nothing. Nora, get Ma to make us a cup of tea, would you?'

'Tea?' Nora yelled. 'You could have been killed! Victoria could have crushed you to death!'

'I'm fine, you great goose,' Erin said. 'Stop your fussing.' She tucked her injured wrist under her other arm, tried to smile, and grimaced again. 'It's all right, Lizzie. I can walk.'

'You sure about that?'

Erin pulled free of Lizzie's arm. 'I've had falls before. Do you think I'm made of bone china? I've been riding since I was a wee snapper.'

'Victoria's OK too, I think,' Hari told them. 'She's shaken, but she's not injured. That was a close one. You were both very lucky.'

'Come on,' Nora said firmly. 'We're going to see Fitzy. He's got to be told!'

Grumbling and wincing from the pain, Erin followed them, leaving Hari to see to the horses. Lizzie was quietly thankful that Victoria hadn't broken her leg – a quick, merciful death by shotgun awaited any circus horse who met with that tragic fate.

They found Fitzy in his caravan. He was looking over some papers, with the oil lamp lit even though it was morning. The weather was so gloomy that only a dim light the colour of old dishwater made it through the windows.

The moment he saw Erin plastered head to foot with mud, he sprang to his feet. 'What happened?'

'There was an accident,' Lizzie explained.

She told him the whole story. While Lizzie spoke, Erin kept her wrist hidden behind her back and fought to keep a brave smile on her face.

'Come on, Erin,' the ringmaster sighed at last. 'Show me.'

Reluctantly, Erin showed him her injured wrist.

ced in sympathy. It was bright red and had like a batch loaf.

Fitzy knuckled his forehead. 'Stupid old man,' he said to himself. 'I should have known better. This is what comes of pushing people too hard.'

'It's not your fault—' Erin tried to say.

'It is absolutely my fault!' Fitzy said, slamming his hand down on the table. 'Don't even try to argue. You must see a doctor, and I am paying, and that's that.'

'But … what about the show?'

'The show is my problem. Nora, Lizzie, take Erin into Kensal Green and find a doctor, would you? I'm going to go and break the news to your mother. I expect she'll skin me alive.'

The three girls set out for the main road, while Fitzy went off in the other direction. Erin looked over her shoulder and watched him go. 'You'd think he'd broken my wrist himself, the way he's carrying on.'

'Can you blame him?' Nora snapped. 'Yesterday he was all practice, practice, practice, and never mind how the horses are acting up. Hari tried to warn him. Malachy too!'

'Is your wrist broken?' Lizzie asked in alarm.

'Probably just a sprain,' said Erin, but the pain in

her eyes told a different story.

As they walked towards the town, Lizzie couldn't help thinking about what would happen now. How could Erin hold Victoria's reins with a broken wrist? Or do a handstand? Even the best doctor in the world couldn't fix her up in time for opening night. And the rain was still coming down like God meant to drown the world again. If Fitzy was ruined and the circus had to close, wherever would she go?

It was a miserable trudge. The cemetery loomed beside the road, but nobody mentioned it. *The girls probably think it's brought us bad luck already*, Lizzie thought. *Who knows, they might even be right.*

They heard the clop of hooves and the creak of wheels coming up behind them. Lizzie worried it might be another funeral procession, but it was – of all things – a farmer's cart, leaving the cemetery gates. A young girl in a simple smock sat at the reins.

'What's she doing in that place?' Nora asked, a little suspicious. *She doesn't even want to say 'cemetery' out loud,* Lizzie noted.

'Who cares?' she said. 'She might know where to find a doctor!' She set off at a run.

'Careful! You know what Ma says about talking to

local folk! They don't like us.'

Lizzie ignored her and flagged down the girl.

The farm girl called 'Whoa, Dandy!' and the shire horse came to a stop.

'He's a beauty,' Lizzie said, admiring him. He was too – a real old piece of England, shaggy and heavy-hoofed, eyeing Lizzie with no show of alarm. *Very different from skittish Victoria*, she thought. *Clearly not every animal is spooked by Kensal Green Cemetery.*

'I suppose he is. Do you like horses, then?' The girl was Lizzie's age, or maybe a little older. She had the sweet, pink-cheeked face of a 'country rose', as Pa Sullivan liked to call the farm girls, but some accident had marked it cruelly. Her skin was covered with tiny scars, as if she'd been peppered with buckshot. And her eyes were dark, as if she'd been crying.

'Love 'em. But I'm no expert. These two, my friends, they ride horses in the circus!' Lizzie pointed to Nora and Erin with pride.

The girl flinched, as if Lizzie had hurt her. 'Don't tease!'

So Lizzie pointed to where the bright colours of the circus tents glimmered from the nearby field. 'We need to find Erin a doctor. She's hurt. One of the horses fell on her.'

'Doctor Gladwell,' the girl said immediately. 'He lives on the other side of Kensal Green. It's a fair walk, though.' As Lizzie's face fell, the girl gave her a half-smile. 'Climb on board if you want. I'll give you a ride there.'

'Thanks!' The three of them scrambled up into the cart, which smelled of old hay and summers long past. 'I'm Lizzie, by the way.'

'I'm Becky. This silly old lump is Dandy.' The shire horse snorted as if he were offended. With a flick of the reins, they set off.

Becky seemed shy and upset, so Lizzie sat beside her and chatted merrily about circus life. The country girl drank it all up, clearly fascinated. 'It sounds quite wonderful,' she said. 'But you're always on the move? You don't have homes anywhere in the world?'

'It's the open road for us!' Nora beamed.

'What happened to your face?' Erin said.

Nora jabbed her hard with her elbow and hissed, 'Erin! You can't just ask people that!'

Becky hesitated. 'I had smallpox.'

'You must have had it bad!' Lizzie said in horror.

Becky shook her head. 'I was lucky. I got better.

But my pa didn't.'

Lizzie snuck a second look at Becky's face. The scars were still quite fresh and some of them were red. She put two and two together in her mind. 'Is that why you were in the cemetery?'

Becky looked at her, bit her lip, then gave a quick nod. 'I wanted to put some flowers on his grave. The wild roses by the old well … they hadn't bloomed when they buried him, but then today the rain brought them out…'

'I'm sure he would have loved them,' Lizzie said. 'Has it been a long time since … since he went?'

'It was only two days ago,' Becky said, her voice catching in her throat.

'I'm sorry,' Lizzie said, meaning it.

'That's awful,' Erin added. She looked guilty for having mentioned Becky's scars in the first place.

Nora gave Becky's shoulders a quick squeeze. 'You poor, poor thing.'

Becky fell silent, keeping her downcast eyes on the road. Lizzie could tell she was crying, but she didn't want to call attention to it.

'It's not easy, losing someone you love,' Lizzie said gently. 'I lost my mum not long ago. She was ill too.'

'Did you have to look after her yourself?' Becky said without looking up.

'Every hour of every day,' Lizzie said. 'My pa … well, he wasn't much use, to tell you the truth. I had to do everything. You feel so lonely, don't you?'

'That's me,' Becky sniffed. 'My mother's long gone. Now my father's gone too. It's like everyone in my life just gets swept away.'

Lizzie wished there was something she could do or say. Poor Becky was more miserable now than before she'd picked them up.

But to her surprise, Becky turned to her with a smile. 'I'm glad I met you, anyway. Doctor Gladwell's a good man. I'm sure he can help your friend.'

'Are you sure this is the right place?' whispered Erin.

Lizzie stood at the end of the gravel driveway, looking up at the house. It reminded her of one of the Kensal Green tombs. Narrow, peaked rooftops loomed against the stormy sky. An immense growth of ivy was gradually strangling the grey flint walls and the door was dark with iron studs, like a mediaeval castle. It even had a ring instead of a proper handle.

'Of course,' Becky said. 'It's a big old house, but the doctor's an important man.'

'I don't want to go in,' Erin declared. 'Let's go somewhere else.'

'Stop being such a baby!' Nora told her.

'Come on, Erin.' Lizzie grabbed her friend by her good hand and dragged her, patiently but firmly, up to the door. Becky wrung her hands, looking this way and that, as if she was embarrassed.

'He probably isn't in,' said Erin.

'Erin, for the last time, will you stop playing up?' Nora grabbed the metal ring and gave three hard knocks. 'There. Now remember your manners and for the love of God wipe your feet or Ma will have our guts for garters.'

From inside the house came the sound of shuffling. Something slid back. There was a pause. Whatever it was slid back again. *That's a spyhole*, thought Lizzie. *Whoever's inside wants to know who's knocking so loud.*

The door creaked open. Lizzie, Nora and Erin all gasped as a wizened, straggly-haired head craned around to peer at them.

'What are you lot after?' the old woman said. An old

black bonnet sat on her head. There was only one tooth in her lower jaw and it stuck up like a tombstone on a crimson hill.

'We wanted to see Doctor Gladwell, if you please, ma'am,' said Lizzie, bobbing in a curtsey.

'Did you indeed, if you please,' the woman said nastily. 'You look like you don't have two ha'pennies to rub together. The doctor's a very busy man. He's got no time for ragamuffins and freeloaders.'

'Right, we'll be off then, cheers.' Erin turned around, but Lizzie held onto her arm.

From further inside came the sound of hearty laughter. 'What are you at, Mrs Crowe, scaring the wits out of children?' It was a pleasant-sounding voice. *Posh*, Lizzie thought, *but the sort of posh you can talk to*.

'It's one of the farm girls, Doctor,' Mrs Crowe called back, 'and some others I ain't never seen before.'

'Then let them in, my dear woman, let them in! Whatever the matter may be with these poor creatures, it won't be helped by leaving them out in the rain, now will it? They'll go all soggy!'

Mrs Crowe scowled at them. 'In you come. Don't waste his time.'

They found Doctor Gladwell sitting by his fire in

a huge parlour room. His bald head was as shiny as a glass paperweight with two puffs of white hair at either side, and he smiled as wide as any of the clowns at Fitzy's Circus. He stood up, revealing himself to be a little man with a round middle. 'Hello!'

Lizzie looked around open-mouthed at all the objects sitting on shelves, and in cases. Stuffed animals, a globe, old medical instruments, more books than you could count … and there, on the desk, a human skull. A real one, missing its lower jaw.

'We'll have a pot of tea, please, quick as you can,' the doctor told Mrs Crowe. The old woman scuttled off with a sour backward glance.

He shook hands with Lizzie, Becky and Nora. His hands were warm and smooth. 'Doctor Josiah Gladwell, at your service. Very pleased to meet you all.' Stopping in front of Erin, he asked, 'And who's this? Too shy to shake hands?'

Erin held out her swollen wrist by way of apology.

Doctor Gladwell took it very gently in his hands. 'I see. And how did this happen?'

'A horse fell on me, Doctor.'

Just for a second, the smile fell. 'Careless. We can't have that. I'm afraid the police will need to have words with the horse's owner.'

'No, it wasn't like that! She's *my* horse. I'm with the circus. My sister and I, we're the Amazing Sullivans.'

'Well I never!' The doctor let out a burst of delighted laughter, like a small boy in short trousers. 'I've never had a patient from a circus before. Now, listen, there will be no charge for my time today – a ticket to the show will suffice! You must tell me all about it.'

With a big smile – Fitzy would be pleased there would be no doctor's bill to pay – Erin did so. She talked excitedly while Doctor Gladwell examined her arm, poking and prodding, and asking if it hurt. Finally, he unrolled a length of bandage and wound it around her arm and shoulder. Even Mrs Crowe coming in with a tray full of tea things didn't stop the chatter.

'You're in luck, my dear,' the doctor said as he stirred his tea. 'Your wrist is badly sprained, but it isn't broken.'

Nora tried to chip in, but Erin wouldn't let her. *She wants the kindly doctor all to herself*, Lizzie thought. She stayed quiet, sipping her tea and looking at a stuffed pine marten that snarled a frozen snarl back at her.

'So I'll be able to perform again soon?' Erin said.

'You will, though I can't say I entirely approve. Call

me an old fuddy-duddy, but the circus sounds like a very dangerous way for young girls to make a living.'

'There's worse out there, Doctor,' Lizzie put in. 'I would have ended up working in a match factory if my dad had had his way. Give me the circus any time.'

The fire made her feel sleepy. It would be so easy to curl up in the armchair and doze off. She had to get up and do something. The tea was finished, so she picked up the tray and went out to find the kitchen.

The hall was much colder, with black and white tiles and a towering grandfather clock ticking loudly. Which of the doors led the way to the kitchen? Lizzie started down the hall, heading for the door that seemed most likely.

'Come away from there, girlie!' snapped a sharp voice. Mrs Crowe snatched the tea tray out of her hands.

As Mrs Crowe touched her, Lizzie felt the dark shadow sweep over her again. A deep chill went through her whole body. *Just like the time with JoJo!* She clutched at the banister to steady herself.

'I'm afraid nobody is allowed in that part of the house,' said Doctor Gladwell, coming out of the parlour. 'The equipment in my laboratory is worth hundreds of pounds.'

'Laboratory?' echoed Lizzie.

'I'm studying something called *bacteria*,' he explained. 'Tiny beasties that make us ill. The better we understand them, the more diseases we can cure. I'm hoping to get smallpox beaten, myself.'

'Could you have made my pa better?' Becky choked out. Lizzie saw tears rolling down her face. 'He died of smallpox.'

'Did he? I'm so sorry. When did he pass away?'

'Two days ago. He's buried up at Kensal Green.'

Doctor Gladwell sighed and patted Becky on both shoulders. 'Dear girl, I'm afraid there is nothing I could have done. We can vaccinate against smallpox, but if it's already taken hold, then one can only pray.'

'Do you think he's in a better place?' Becky whispered.

'I'm sure of it. And I promise you, I will not rest until that filthy disease is wiped out.'

'Doctor,' said Mrs Crowe in a voice like a croak, 'your next appointment is here. Waiting. Very patiently, I might add.'

'Right! Now, Miss Erin, you must rest your arm for at least two weeks. No gadding about. Understood?'

'Yes, Doctor,' Erin said with a wide smile. 'Thank you.'

As they bustled to the door, with Mrs Crowe all but pushing them out, the doctor waved. 'Just leave my ticket at the box office, and I'll make sure I come to the show! Cheerio, all!'

The next appointment was two men in canal workers' clothes, sitting outside on a garden bench. Their caps were pulled down against the bright sunlight.

Sunlight? Lizzie looked up, saw blue sky and laughed in happy relief. 'Finally. About bloomin' time! It's stopped raining!'

'Well,' sighed Erin, looking down at her sling, 'that's one less thing to worry about. But two whole weeks! What are we going to tell Fitzy?'

CHAPTER 4

To Lizzie, who had grown up in the slum they called Rat's Castle, the countryside was like a foreign country. Right now it looked like something out of a fairy tale, glittering in the bright sunshine. Drops of rain hung diamond-bright on every leaf and bloom. She had a crazy urge to go running through the fields, trampling the long grass down and leaving a wake behind her.

'Come back to my farmhouse,' Becky suggested hopefully. 'Tilly gives lovely fresh milk, and it's on the way.'

'We should get back to the circus,' Nora said hesitantly. 'Fitzy's expecting us back soon.'

'Just one cup of milk? It won't take long.'

Lizzie suspected that Becky didn't often have the chance to ask visitors back. 'We'd love to,' she said firmly, answering for all of them. That settled that.

Becky drove them to her farm. Some of the fences were in disrepair. Chickens ran to and fro in the yard, pecking at the muck between the cobblestones. 'Oh, no,' Becky moaned. 'The hens have got out again.'

It looked half-abandoned for a working farm. 'Isn't anyone else here?' Lizzie asked doubtfully.

'There's only me now that Pa's gone,' Becky said.

'You take care of a whole farm by yourself? You must be run off your feet!'

Becky shooed the chickens back into their enclosure. Nora and Erin ran around helping as best they could, while Lizzie made sure the captive hens didn't get out again. Once they were all caught, Becky bashed the loose panel back into place with her elbow. 'Right,' she said, dusting off her hands. 'Let's get that milk.'

In the welcome shade of the cowshed, Lizzie watched in fascination as Becky's strong, scarred hands milked Tilly into a tin bucket.

'Have you never seen a cow milked before?' Becky teased.

Lizzie laughed. 'I'm a city girl! They gave us weak beer when I was little, not milk.'

'Beer?' Erin and Nora said together.

'Couldn't have water, 'cause of the cholera. Beer was safer.'

Jets of milk squirted into the bucket, making a rattling sound. It looked creamy and delicious. Once there was plenty to go around, Becky passed them all cups. Lizzie felt a bit odd about drinking something that had been inside an animal moments before, especially as it was still warm, but she soon found herself gulping it down greedily.

'You're really good at that milking,' she told Becky. 'I wouldn't know which end to start with.'

'My pa taught me everything I know,' Becky said, sighing. 'I miss him so much.'

'You must do, you poor thing.' Lizzie hardly knew what to say. What could she possibly say to a girl whose father was only two days dead? Becky couldn't even be used to it yet.

Becky wiped her eyes. 'I do stupid things. Last night I laid the table for two, just like I always used to. I wasn't even thinking. And this morning, just after the cock crowed, I lay in bed and wondered why Pa wasn't shouting at me to get up. I forgot he was dead. How can that happen?'

'Well, I think he'd be proud of you, running the farm like this all by yourself,' Lizzie said. Erin and Nora nodded, milk moustaches on both of their upper lips.

Becky shrugged. 'What else can I do? The animals need me. My father didn't keep this place running just for me to let it go to rack and ruin, did he?'

'But it must be so hard!' Nora said.

'There's no sense in feeling sorry for myself,' Becky said, though tears were rolling down her cheeks. 'That won't get the milk to market, will it? You needn't feel sorry for me, neither. I deserve … I deserve this.'

Lizzie caught hold of Becky's shoulders and gave her a hug. 'That's a load of nonsense!'

'It's not,' Becky sobbed into Lizzie's sleeve. 'You don't understand. He caught the smallpox from *me*. He'd never have been ill if it wasn't for me.'

'That's not your fault!'

'But I got better … and he … he died…'

Lizzie held the girl tight as she wept. Nobody else had done this for her, that much was obvious. Nora and Erin looked on with sympathetic faces.

'I just wish I could speak to him again!' Becky pulled

back, wiping away tears.

Nora suddenly leaned in. 'If you *could* speak to him, what would you say?' she asked.

A little startled, Becky thought for a moment. 'I'd ask him to forgive me. For the smallpox. And tell him I love him.' She sniffed. 'But I'll never get to speak to him again, will I?'

Nora was giving Lizzie a strange look – keen-eyed and excited. 'Maybe Lizzie could speak to him for you.'

'What?' Lizzie spluttered.

'Lizzie's psychic,' said Erin, in a casual way that made Lizzie want to shove her off the hay bale she was sitting on. This was horrible. What if they gave Becky false hope?

Becky stared at her, dumbfounded.

'I'm the circus fortune-teller,' Lizzie said apologetically. 'I can, sort of, see into the future.'

'There's no "sort of" about it!' Nora said. 'Lizzie's just being modest. She's got powers!'

'But I ain't never talked to a...' She had to say the word. 'To a ghost!'

'You've never tried,' said Erin, swigging her milk and raising her eyebrow.

Lizzie clenched her teeth and glared at Erin. 'I

don't even believe in ghosts,' she hissed. 'Dead people go up to Heaven, they don't stick around down here for a chat!'

'But Lizzie, your visions have never been wrong yet,' Nora said. 'If anyone can talk to the dead, it's you. I think you should try.'

'You must!' Becky fell on her knees, to Lizzie's amazement. 'I'm begging you. Please try.'

Put on the spot as she was, Lizzie had to at least consider it. Could she speak to a dead person? She could try, perhaps, but she wasn't even sure *how*. Apart from palm-reading, which Madame Aurora had shown her how to do, her visions just happened. She didn't have any control over them.

So what on earth should she do? Wander around in the cemetery and knock on the gravestones, hoping someone answered? Sit in a circle like a spirit medium and ask if there was anybody there? Knock once for yes, twice for no…?

'Please?' Becky said, wide-eyed.

Lizzie knew she couldn't refuse. 'All right,' she said. 'You did us a good turn, helping us get to the doctor and all, so I'll do it. I'll try to speak to your father.'

Before Becky could give her another enormous hug,

Lizzie quickly added, 'But not now, OK? There isn't time. We've got to get the twins back to the circus.'

'Fitzy will burst a blood vessel if we're not back soon,' Nora agreed. 'Wait, Becky. I've got something for you.' She fished a slip of yellow paper out of her pocket. 'Come along to the show tonight!'

'A circus ticket?' Becky said in delight.

'On the house. Can you come? I know you're busy here, so…'

'I'll come! Just try and stop me!'

'Come to my tent before the show,' Lizzie told her, 'and I'll see what I can do. I can't promise anything. But I'll try.' She paused as a thought struck her. 'Bring something that belonged to your pa. It might help make a connection.'

After all, she thought as she left the farmhouse, *I can't read a dead man's palm, can I*? Even the thought made her shudder.

Back at the circus the three girls gathered outside Fitzy's caravan, looking nervously at one another, not wanting to go in.

Eventually Lizzie spoke up. 'Let's get it over with.'

They knocked.

Fitzy came out immediately with Malachy behind him. He saw Erin's sling, and his face fell. 'Is it broken?'

'The doctor said it was just a bad sprain,' said Erin.

'Then you can still perform?'

Erin shook her head sadly. 'I've got to rest up while it heals. I can't ride.'

Fitzy covered his face with his hands. Then he parted his fingers so he could see through them. 'How long?' came his muffled voice.

'Two weeks.'

'That's impossible. Can't be done.' Fitzy suddenly started walking off through the circus. The girls and Malachy ran to follow him.

He spoke quickly as he walked: 'The posters have already gone up. They're plastered all over the town. I spent a fortune on them, like a fool! Can't be helped now, it's done, it's spent.' He spun on the spot and kept talking, walking backwards, waving his hands. 'You two are on the posters! The Sullivan Twins! I can't do the show with just *one*! What if people want their money back, eh? What am I supposed to tell them?'

Lizzie had never seen him in such a panic. 'The

circus will be ruined,' he mumbled. 'I can't let that happen … there must be something we can do!'

Then he stopped. He looked from Lizzie to Erin and back to Lizzie. 'Yes,' he said softly. 'It just might work…'

'What?' Lizzie said, totally confused now.

'It's the only solution,' Fitzy said. 'We can't do the show without two girls. You're about Erin's height. So you'll have to go on in her place.'

Lizzie's mouth fell open.

'Congratulations, Lizzie.' Fitzy patted her on the back. 'You just became the new Sullivan sister. Better get some riding practice in!'

CHAPTER 5

It was the craziest idea Lizzie had ever heard.

'But Fitzy, I barely know how to ride a horse. I can't do handstands and tricks on horseback like Erin does! I'd break me neck!'

'I can teach you,' Nora said. 'You'll pick it up pretty quick. After all, I was only four when I first learned. If I can do it, you can!'

'But the first show is tonight! I can't pick it up *that* quick.'

Malachy tugged at his father's brightly coloured coat. 'Don't do this, Pop. It's not fair on Lizzie.'

'Oh, I know it's a lot to ask,' Fitzy said,

tucking his thumbs through his braces. 'But they don't call her the Magnificent Lizzie Brown for nothing, do they?'

'Pop, be serious. Erin's already hurt. Lizzie could get hurt too. We should play it safe instead of taking all these unnecessary risks.'

For a moment, Fitzy looked like he might buckle under. He rubbed his forehead and looked very tired. There hadn't been much of the old familiar sparkle in his eyes lately, and he had been putting in too many late nights.

'I owe a lot of money, son,' he said, in a guilty voice that hurt Lizzie's heart. 'More than I've let on, to tell you the truth. If I could go back and do things differently, I would … but it's too late.'

Fitzy had always been a risk-taker. Lizzie knew that. He'd taken a risk when he first gave her a job in his circus. If he hadn't, she'd probably be dead now, or slaving in a match factory with phosphorus burns on her fingers, heading for an early grave. Seeing him now, so sad and defeated, she knew she had to do her best to help. She could take a risk too, for his sake.

'I'll do it!' she said.

Fitzy glanced up, and from deep inside the black circles of his pupils a tiny gleam shone like a spark in the night. 'Good girl.'

Lizzie's one and only training session was in the show tent, on firm sawdust-strewn ground. There would be no more rehearsals outside in the wet. Everyone had quietly left before Lizzie arrived, to give her some privacy.

They don't want to see me falling off and landing on my face, she thought darkly. *Can't blame 'em.*

Hari led Albert into the ring. 'He's the better-behaved of the two new horses, so you can ride him,' said Nora. 'Now, he's used to having me stand up on his back, so he won't buck you off. Will you, my lovely?'

Lizzie rubbed Albert's neck. 'We're going to have to learn to trust each other,' she whispered. Albert whickered and dipped his head in what looked surprisingly like a nod. Erin checked the reins and the special saddle. 'All set.'

'Right, then,' said Nora. 'Let's get you up. Do you need a hand, or...'

Lizzie took the reins along with a little tuft of mane, put her left foot into the stirrup and pushed herself up with her right leg. She swung her right leg up and over, coming to rest squarely in the saddle.

'Good!' Nora patted her leg. 'How do you feel?'

'Not too bad,' Lizzie admitted.

'Let's try a stand-up. Pop your feet out of the stirrups.'

With Nora patiently talking her through it, Lizzie was able to draw her leg up and rest on her shin, then put one foot on the horse's back followed by the other, so that she was squatting.

She felt ridiculous. *Who's going to pay to see this?* Even with Albert standing stock-still, she was wobbling around wildly.

'Now rise to a standing position,' Nora said. 'Slowly does it. Imagine there's an invisible cord connecting you to the sky. It helps you balance.'

Strangely, it worked. Lizzie straightened her legs. 'I'm standing up!' she said. 'I'm doing it! Blimey.'

'It's a start,' said Erin, clapping.

Lizzie swallowed, feeling like there was a lump of fear stuck in her throat. 'It's a long way down.' She struggled to keep her balance. Albert shook his head and snorted, as if a fly was bothering him.

'Just get used to standing for now,' Nora said, but Erin pushed past her. 'Try one leg!' she said. 'Go on! It's easier than you think.'

'Erin!' Nora was furious.

'What? She's got to learn.'

'I'm teaching her, not you!'

Lizzie stared at her quivering feet as the twins bickered. She lifted one foot hesitantly, felt she was about to fall, and put it straight back down again. In her imagination she heard crowds jeering and booing.

'Try putting your arms out,' Nora suggested.

Slowly, Lizzie raised her arms, trembling like a willow in the wind, until she was standing in a cross shape. Albert shifted beneath her and she yelped and dropped her arms again.

'Maybe if Lizzie just looks decorative, and you do all the stunts?' Erin suggested.

Nora wrinkled her nose. 'That'll have to do, won't it?'

Lizzie looked out at the empty stalls. Tonight the tent would be packed. She was going to be a laughing stock. She knew it.

Albert wasn't helping, either. He stamped a hoof

and whinnied loudly. Suddenly Lizzie was sure he was going to throw her. She dropped down to a squat and threw her legs back over his sides, clinging on for dear life.

That just made Albert worse. He fretted, not quite rearing up, but fidgeting and tossing his head.

'He don't like me,' Lizzie said, sagging her shoulders. 'This ain't ever going to work.'

Hari appeared at her side. He stroked Albert's nose and crooned softly into his ear. 'There, now. Easy, now. You're a good boy, yes you are.' Instantly Albert was calmer, and nuzzled Hari's ear in turn, making him giggle.

'Maybe you should get this dress on instead of me,' Lizzie pouted.

'It's not that he doesn't like you,' Hari told her. 'He's nervous because *you're* nervous. Do what I did.'

Lizzie leaned over and whispered to Albert as Hari had done. It worked.

'See how much better he is now?' Hari smiled at Lizzie encouragingly. 'Animals have strong intuition. Even if you're scared up there, you can't show Albert, or he'll pick up on it and act scared too. You have to let him know that you trust him to keep you safe.'

* * *

Lizzie tried to put her upcoming performance out of her mind. She was still the circus fortune-teller and there was work to do. The penny gaffs and sideshows always opened up before the main show went on, to help pull in the crowds.

She hurried to her mystic tent, just in time for the start of her shift. As she pulled on her robes, she wondered what Fitzy would have done if it had been *her* who was injured. There weren't any other psychics who could take her place. Lizzie lit some incense to give the stuffy tent an exotic atmosphere.

Her first customer arrived within minutes. She was a broad-shouldered young woman in a shawl, with tired eyes. In her arms she held a baby wrapped in a grubby blue blanket, while a toddler with a runny nose clutched at her skirts.

'It smells funny in here,' the child said.

'Don't be rude, Tommy! I'm sorry – do you mind if he comes in with me? Their dad's away at sea, and there's nobody to mind 'em, so…'

'It's fine,' Lizzie said with a pained smile.

'Ball!' Tommy lunged for Lizzie's crystal ball with

his sticky fingers. Before she could snatch it away from him, he'd smeared it with heaven only knew what.

'Don't worry,' Lizzie told his dismayed mother. 'It'll keep him happy if he has something pretty to play with.'

The reading began. As Lizzie traced her finger down the woman's line of life, she saw images from her past: her wedding day to a tattooed sailor man, the crowd gathered around her mother's deathbed, the day Tommy was born and she'd nearly died of a fever. When Lizzie glimpsed the future, it was Christmas. The woman's husband was proudly cuddling a newborn baby under the tree while an older Tommy bashed a wooden train against the furniture and his little sibling rolled about on the rug.

When Lizzie told her about the baby, the woman smiled bravely. 'Another one? Well … the more the merrier, eh?' After she'd paid, she paused on the way out. 'Did you see if it was a boy or a girl?'

Lizzie shook her head. 'Sorry.'

'Never mind. It'll be a lovely surprise, I'm sure.'

The next customer was a nervous, skinny young man who kept cracking his knuckles. Before Lizzie could say a word, he burst out: 'I'm very much in love.'

'That's nice. How can I help?'

'My beloved … she is beyond compare. No words could possibly do her justice.'

Lizzie said, a little tersely, 'I don't do love potions, if that's what you're after.'

'Certainly not!' The man swallowed; his Adam's apple stuck out like a knuckle. 'I wish to propose to her.'

'Look, chum,' Lizzie said, dropping the mystic airs completely, 'if you want to propose, why not just go ahead and do it? Jump in with both feet. That's what she wants.'

The man knotted his fingers together, shoved them in his lap and pulled a strained face. 'But what if she says no? What, then? I lie awake at night, I toss and I turn … I tell myself not to be a fool and simply to ask her, and then I imagine myself rejected, and I cannot bear it, for life would be unthinkable then.'

He doesn't need a psychic, Lizzie thought. *He wants a good hard kick in the backside!* But she forced herself to smile. He was a customer, even if he was an idiot.

'I can try to see your future,' she said. 'Give me your hand.'

He shut his eyes and held his open palm out. Lizzie

found the right line and traced it. Instantly pictures leaped into her mind.

'Good news!' she said. 'I can see you, walking down the aisle of a country church, smiling fit to bust. There's a beautiful young girl by your side.'

'Truly?' He gave a gasping laugh as if he'd just been told he'd been spared from the gallows. 'We are to be wed?'

'She's lovely, sir. Dressed all in white, flowers in her long black hair … she's the happiest girl in the world!'

He smiled a dreamy smile, then suddenly his eyes flew open and the smile vanished. 'Black hair? But my Julia is blonde!'

Lizzie ushered him out of the tent as quickly as she could. 'You both looked ever so happy,' she assured the confused young man.

The next customer was Becky. She peeped shyly into the tent, only coming inside when Lizzie beckoned her. She was clutching something tightly.

'If you'd been dressed like that when I met you, I'd have been too scared to speak!' Becky whispered. 'You look like a gypsy out of a fairy tale.'

'It's only for show,' Lizzie said. 'Did you bring something of your pa's?'

'Yes!' Becky opened her hand. A metal ornament gleamed there, circular and decorated with holes all the way through, with a cross in the centre and a loop at the top for a strap to go through. Lizzie had seen them many times, hanging from the harnesses of shire horses – including the one she'd met yesterday.

'A horse brass?'

'He loved Dandy,' Becky explained. 'Horse brasses usually come in pairs, so when he died, we buried him with one of Dandy's. I kept the other one.'

Lizzie had to admit it was a perfect choice. A matched set of brasses, one here, the other in Becky's father's grave with his dead body! If anything could make a connection, this surely could.

If.

Lizzie gently took it from her. Becky watched with such a hopeful look on her face that Lizzie wondered if maybe, just this once, it was worth telling a white lie. She could pretend to see Becky's dad's spirit and say something comforting. The girl would be none the wiser.

She held the horse brass in one hand and stroked it with the fingers of the other, as if it had been a living person's palm. Then, to her astonishment, an image began to appear in her mind, first as a blurry outline, then as a human form walking towards her. The closer he came, the clearer his image grew.

'Can you see him?' Becky asked, breathless.

'Your pa … was he quite a strong bloke, with a bushy beard?'

'Yes!'

'He's wearing a cloth cap and big work boots. And a waistcoat. Now he's smiling and holding a hand up. There's a scar across his nose.'

'That's him!' Becky couldn't sit still with excitement. 'Paul Wardle's bulldog nipped him on the nose when I was little. It couldn't be anyone else!'

He was speaking now. The voice echoed through Lizzie's mind:

'*Tell her I'm at peace, miss, if you'd be so kind. I love her dearly and I couldn't be prouder.*'

Lizzie repeated those exact words. Becky laughed and wept at the same time.

'*I know she'll look after the farm,*' the spirit told Lizzie. It was always so strange, hearing another voice in the inside of her mind where only her own thoughts usually were. '*Tell her when it gets tough, to remember that I'm watching over her every day. Give Dandy a kiss for me.*' The figure tugged at his cap, by way of saying thank you, and faded away.

When Lizzie had passed on everything Becky's father had told her, she tried to give the horse brass back.

'No, you keep it!' Becky insisted. 'It's a present. You've been so lovely. I know he's with me now, not just as a memory, but really there! How can I ever thank you enough?'

As she hugged Becky, Lizzie saw a new, powerful vision in her mind.

It was night. Mist crawled around her ankles. She was standing in a graveyard, among the looming monuments and headstones. From close by came the scrape, rattle, scrape of someone digging.

She tried to block the vision out, but it just grew stronger.

She was rushing towards a freshly dug grave. As it opened up to swallow her, she heard the terrible howl of a gigantic hound, and next moment, a piercing scream.

CHAPTER 6

There was hardly any time before Lizzie was due to perform with Nora on horseback. She rushed off to the Sullivans' caravan, with the vision still haunting her.

Why would she see a graveyard? It had to be something to do with Kensal Green, but why would someone be digging there at night? And that scream … it made her skin crawl.

No time to worry about that now! she told herself. *There's bigger fish to fry.*

Erin and Ma Sullivan were waiting for her at their trailer.

'Come on then, my love,' Ma said. 'Let's make a

Sullivan girl of you.'

First, Lizzie's hair had to be dyed red with henna, or the audience would never take her for a Sullivan twin. It was messy, and the henna smelled like overcooked spinach, but the effect was astonishing. Lizzie's brown hair blazed a coppery red.

Now it was time to get dressed. Erin's white costume, spangled with sequins, was laid out and ready. Lizzie quickly slipped it on.

She stared at herself in a full-length mirror. The dress clung to her like a cloud, as light as a wisp of cotton. Sequins flashed and dazzled as she moved, catching the light from the oil lamp.

'Crikey,' she said, turning this way and that. 'I don't half feel glamorous in your togs, Erin.'

'We're not done yet.' Ma Sullivan sat her down and perched on a stool opposite. 'Hold still.'

Erin looked on approvingly as her mother used a soft brush to daub Lizzie's cheeks with rouge. It smelled like roses. 'This is the real stuff,' Ma Sullivan assured her. 'All the most fashionable Parisian dancing girls wear it.'

As a finishing touch, she added some shimmering colour to Lizzie's eyelids and warmed up her lips with some crimson make-up.

'Hair next.' With practised skill, she gathered Lizzie's unruly hair up and braided it into a long plait. With a silver fastening at the end, it looked just like Nora's.

Ma Sullivan stepped back to admire her work. 'Ah, Liz, if I didn't know better I'd say I'd had triplets all them years ago. You're the spit of me own girls.'

Erin gave her a quick, fierce hug. 'You're a wonder, so you are. Thanks for stepping in like this.'

'Aww, you all took me in and looked after me,' Lizzie said, feeling strangely shy. 'I always felt like part of the family. So I'm happy to pretend to be a Sullivan, if it helps you out!'

On the far side of the circus ring, opposite the main entrance where the public came in, was an archway made from brightly painted wood. This was the performers' entrance and exit.

A beaded curtain hung across the archway making a glittering barrier. The lighting inside the show tent meant the archway was always dark, so performers could take their places and wait for their cues. It was like the wings in a theatre.

Lizzie waited there in the shadows, watching the show start. Most of the seats were full. Fitzy, she was glad to see, was on top form, firing off jokes and making the crowd roar with laughter. What a relief it must be to have pulled in a decent audience!

The Boissets were the opening act. After some spectacular trapeze routines that had the crowd gasping, it was time for Dru to perform on the high wire. He and Collette were debuting a new routine. Collette cycled out onto the rope on her penny farthing, drawing wild applause. She pedalled back and forth, then Dru came towards her from the opposite end, using an umbrella as a balancing pole.

Lizzie's heart was in her mouth. Why, oh why would Dru never use a safety net?

Dru and Collette play-acted the parts of a pedestrian and a cyclist meeting in a narrow lane, with neither one willing to step aside for the other. Dru angrily hopped up and down, the rope twanging as he did, then somersaulted on the spot. In response, Collette climbed up onto her bicycle seat and pretended to shake her fists at him.

The blend of comedy and daring high-wire action

was causing a sensation with the crowd, but Lizzie felt sick with nerves. She knew she shouldn't watch, but privately she was afraid of what might happen if she didn't.

As a finale, Dru solved the stalemate by climbing up the penny-farthing's huge wheel and balancing on his sister's shoulders. He bowed, and the audience went wild.

The band played a jolly oom-pah tune. Lizzie pressed herself against the side of the tunnel as the clowns came running past her, through the beaded curtain and out into the bright light of the circus ring. She gave them a thumbs up for luck.

JoJo staggered past after them, clutching his stomach. Lizzie caught a whiff of something nasty, like sour sweat.

Nora came up next to her. She'd been warming up the horses while Lizzie had been transformed into a Sullivan twin. 'Don't fret, Lizzie. You'll do fine.'

'What's JoJo doing out there?' Lizzie whispered. 'He's meant to be resting!'

'He didn't want to let Fitzy down,' Nora said.

The clown routine was set in a bakery. Didi, the serious whiteface clown, was bossing the others about, demanding they work faster. The more they tried to follow his mimed orders, the more chaos resulted. Clowns carrying pies crashed into each other and, as messy mock fights broke out, pies were slipped in and sat on.

JoJo was the Auguste clown, the zaniest of the lot. He usually capered around being the rebel, making trouble for Didi. Tonight, though, he was just lurching around the ring, holding his belly and sometimes falling to his knees.

Didi pelted him with pies and aimed kicks at his baggy bottom while the band played trombone parps. The audience ate it up. Some of them were falling out of their seats from laughing so hard. All throughout the act, Lizzie could see JoJo grimacing under his painted-on smile.

'They don't know,' Lizzie said, alarmed. 'They think it's all part of the act. Poor JoJo must be feeling terrible.'

'He's a trouper, though,' Nora said. 'He's had his clown face on since he came out of his trailer this morning! I expect he's raring to get back to work.'

All too soon, the clowns came back out and Fitzy was introducing the next act: 'Two incredible young equestrian performers.'

Lizzie's stomach did flip-flops. They'd all be watching her.

Nora gave her a quick squeeze. 'You'll be fantastic.'

Hari came up behind them, leading Albert and Victoria. Lizzie looked into Albert's calm brown eyes.

'Please show your appreciation…' Fitzy was saying. There was a roll on the drums.

Lizzie stroked Albert's nose. 'Look after me. Please?'

Albert whinnied softly. Lizzie took a deep breath and mounted his back.

'… for the Amazing Sullivan Twins!' Fitzy finished.

To the sound of a fanfare, Lizzie and Nora rode out into the dazzling lights of the sawdust ring. A sea of faces surrounded her.

I can do this.

Lizzie forced herself to smile. She steadily rose to a standing position, holding Albert's reins firmly.

Meanwhile, Nora was already on one leg, cantering around the ring and waving at the crowd. There was a smattering of applause, but it was all for Nora.

It didn't matter. All Lizzie had to do was look pretty and not fall off. Despite the hundreds of people watching, she felt her confidence rise.

I trust you, Albert, she thought. She gave the reins a twitch and Albert obediently trotted forwards, with Lizzie still standing upright.

'Bravo!' shouted a man at the front of the stalls. Was he mocking her? Lizzie didn't dwell on it. *I'm doing my best. What more can I do?*

Most of the crowd only had eyes for Nora, and Lizzie was fine with that. Nora went through her routine without a single mistake, flipping onto her hands and back onto her feet, doing a pirouette on Victoria's back, and even catching the juggling clubs that Lizzie threw to her. The crowd clapped, but the act wasn't captivating them the way it did when Erin performed with her sister.

Nora came thundering around the ring for the big finale. Usually, she and Erin would leap through the air, do a mid-air splits and land on each other's horse. Lizzie wasn't ready to attempt jumping off, let alone landing on a horse. She quickly dismounted and held Albert's reins, leaving the saddle empty for Nora to land on.

She crossed her fingers as Nora rode towards her. A drumroll began. Even without Erin, the leap would an impressive stunt. The crowd *had* to like it, surely.

Then a rude voice rang out, aimed at Lizzie: 'GET BACK ON YER 'ORSE, DARLIN'!' A few laughs followed and Lizzie's cheeks burned with embarrasment.

Now Victoria was whinnying and rearing up. The shouting had spooked her. Nora desperately tried to make her leap anyway, but it was a disaster. She toppled from Victoria's back and fell with a sharp cry, scrambling quickly out of the way in case the horse toppled over onto her.

'Oh, no!' Lizzie murmured. Hari quickly ran out to pacify Victoria. Nora fled off through the archway, choking back tears.

All Lizzie could do was trudge after her. The band quickly struck up a marching tune to close the act, but not quickly enough to drown out the booing.

It was only one or two voices at first, then others joined in: 'Boo!' 'Call that an act?' 'Get off!' Lizzie felt herself shrivelling up like a salted slug.

Once safely backstage, Lizzie pressed her back against the wooden archway and tried not to cry. The lion was being led out now. Good. That would entertain this awful crowd.

'Lizzie, it's OK,' Malachy said from the shadows

beside her.

'You must be joking,' Lizzie sniffed. 'Didn't you hear 'em? I've never been so mortified.'

'I know the act got messed up. But at least you went out there! None of them can say they didn't get what they paid for, even if it wasn't what they were expecting. We advertised the Sullivan twins, and they got the Sullivan twins. Pop kept his word. That's all that matters.'

Once the show was over and the last of the audience members had filtered out into the night, Fitzy called all the performers back into the show tent for the traditional after-show chat.

It was all part of Fitzy's style. If any performance hadn't been up to scratch, he'd let you know while it was still fresh in your mind, so you could do something to fix it. But there was always humour and respect. Fitzy would never humiliate anyone in his circus in front of the others, no matter how badly they'd screwed up.

Lizzie and Nora still sat uncomfortably, waiting for him to turn his attention their way – as he surely would. *The audience booed! Had anyone in Fitzy's Circus ever been booed before?*

'Lizzie, you're a trouper. Thank you for stepping in at the last minute.' Fitzy whistled and puffed out his cheeks. 'You had a tough crowd tonight, though, girls. I think some of them had had a bit too much to drink. Don't take it to heart, eh?'

'OK, Fitzy,' they said together.

Lizzie had to smile. Now she and Nora were speaking the same words at the same time, just like Erin!

'Hari, see what you can do to calm Victoria down. That wretched horse will be the death of— I'm sorry, sir, the show's finished.'

Everyone turned to look. Doctor Gladwell was poking his head around the entrance. 'And what a rip-roaring show it was!' he said. 'Sorry to interrupt. I was wondering if I could check young Erin's arm.'

Lizzie leaped to her feet. 'This is Doctor Josiah Gladwell, Fitzy! He helped us. We left a ticket for him.'

Fitzy strode over and shook the doctor's hand, pumping it up and down. 'Doctor. Welcome. We're all in your debt. Erin, let's be having you.'

After the doctor had gently checked the swelling and moved Erin's wrist back and forth a little, he patted her on the shoulder. 'Good girl. You did what you were told, didn't you?'

'I did, Doctor,' Erin said proudly. 'Lots of rest, no larking about.'

'She's healing up a treat, sir,' the doctor told Fitzy.

Relief shone out of the ringmaster's face. But then he looked puzzled. 'What's the matter now?'

Doctor Gladwell was peering over his glasses at JoJo. 'That clown, there. How long has he been ill?'

'A couple of days, possibly longer. Why?'

'I need to remove his make-up.' The doctor stepped forward, and was startled when the clowns closed ranks around JoJo.

'You'll do no such thing, mate,' said Didi, sounding cold and menacing.

Fitzy cleared his throat. 'Doctor, it is very much against circus custom to remove a clown's make-up without his permission.'

'It certainly is,' Didi said. The clowns muttered in agreement.

'Then I must ask the gentleman to do it himself,' Doctor Gladwell said with a shrug.

The clowns angrily rallied around. 'You can't do that!' Didi said. 'It's his face. You can't make him take it off!'

'I'm afraid it's a matter of the utmost importance,' the doctor persisted.

JoJo looked up at Fitzy through pained eyes. 'It's nothing,' he protested. 'Just a few spots, that's all.'

'JoJo,' Fitzy said softly, 'please do as the doctor says.'

JoJo reached for a sponge and water with trembling hands. He wiped a stripe of white makeup from his forehead.

The clowns surrounding him gasped and backed away as they saw what was underneath. 'Mate,' spluttered Rice Pudding Pete, 'why didn't you say? You could have told us!'

JoJo coughed. 'Didn't want to be a bother,' he wheezed.

The clown's skin was covered with ugly round bumps with little dimples in the centre. It was the same disease that had left Becky's face scarred ... and had killed her father. No wonder JoJo had been suffering. He'd worn his thick make-up to hide the signs.

'I thought as much. This man has smallpox,' Doctor Gladwell said. 'He's gravely ill.'

Lizzie remembered the vision of death she'd seen when she touched JoJo. Ma Sullivan was shaking her head and whispering something to Pa. She looked like she badly needed to say 'I told you so'.

'He has to be kept away from other people and given treatment immediately. Your whole cast could be infected.'

'Right. Didi, get JoJo to hospital right away.'

'Oh, you needn't do that,' Doctor Gladwell said. 'The nearest hospital is miles away. I can take him back to my house with me. I've been immunized, so I can give him the treatment he needs.'

'Are you sure?' Fitzy looked stunned. 'Isn't it a terrible imposition?'

'My dear sir, it's the least I can do. A circus is just the sort of fun we need in this gloomy old place. Let me take JoJo home, and if you like, any of your cast who haven't had smallpox before can be immunized. What do you say to that?'

'I say thank you,' Fitzy burst out. 'Thank you ten thousand times over.' He shook the doctor's hand again, so hard he nearly rattled the little man's glasses off. Then he clicked his heels together. 'Right, you lot. Anyone who hasn't had the smallpox yet, meet here tomorrow at ten to sort out your immunizations. No excuses!'

* * *

The Penny Gaff Gang – Lizzie, Dru, Hari, Malachy, Nora and Erin – lingered in the show tent after everyone else had left.

'You looked *très belle* up there on your horse tonight,' Dru teased Lizzie. 'I think your new career suits you. But oh, how I miss your brown hair.'

'I'll do it in me mystic veil next time, so they can't see me face!' Lizzie squirmed, still feeling the sting of humiliation. 'I don't know how you lot can stand it, having all them people staring at you.'

Erin laughed. 'That's the fun of it! Being in the glare of the lights, the crowd eating out of the palm of your hand…'

'Rather you than me. Give me my nice quiet tent any day of the week.'

Malachy banged his walking stick on the ground. 'Silence! I hereby call this meeting of the Penny Gaff Gang to order.' He gestured. 'Lizzie Brown, O prophet of things to come, you have something to tell us, don't you?'

'Yeah, I do, actually.' Lizzie stood up. 'I've had a

vision. It was a cemetery … Kensal Green, I'm sure of it. There was digging after dark, and an open grave, and a dog howling, and then a girl screaming.'

'Who were you reading for?' Malachy asked.

'Nobody. It just came to me. I think the power's sending me a warning.'

Nora and Erin's eyes went very wide. They looked terrified. Lizzie could guess what they were worried about, but it wasn't going to stop her.

'Something's going on up at the cemetery,' she said boldly, 'and I want to go and investigate. Who's with me?'

CHAPTER 7

'Lizzie, you can't mean it!' spluttered Nora. Her voice fell to a whisper. 'Go to the *cemetery*?'

'Don't you think we've had bad luck here already?' Erin curled her lip like a frightened horse, glancing fearfully about. 'What in the world's got into you?'

'You're sure it was one of your visions?' Hari said reluctantly. 'You weren't ... perhaps ... imagining things?'

Lizzie gave him a withering look. 'You think I *want* to go up there? Of course I don't! But we all know I don't see these visions without a reason. Come on, have I led you wrong yet?'

'Not so far,' said Dru, giving his trademark shrug. 'I wouldn't be here if it wasn't for your visions.'

The Penny Gaff Gang were silent for a moment, remembering when Dru had been falsely accused of being the Phantom. If it hadn't been for Lizzie's visions unmasking the real culprit, Dru could have been hanged.

'So there's something wrong, and it needs putting right. Who's coming?' Lizzie looked around at Erin and Nora's frightened faces. 'Are we the Penny Gaff Gang or aren't we?'

'Lizzie, it could be dangerous,' Nora insisted.

'Whatever's going on, it can't be more dangerous than the Phantom, can it? And we beat him!'

Nora teased a pinch of her hair nervously. 'The Phantom was only a man. He could only ever hurt your body. But the beast that's supposed to dwell in Kensal Green Cemetery can devour your very *soul*.'

'"Devour your very soul,"' Lizzie said cynically. 'Did your mum tell you that?'

'Don't you say nothing against our ma!' Erin said, leaping to her feet.

'I'm not!' Lizzie quickly assured her. 'I just don't believe in the, you know … oh, cobblers to it! I don't believe in the Devil's Hound! There. I've said it.'

Nora and Erin glanced at one another. 'I hope you don't have reason to eat them rash words, Lizzie,' Nora said seriously.

'Many's the proud girl who's been brought low by mocking what she don't rightly understand,' added Erin.

'All right, you're not coming! I get it!' Lizzie flung her hands up. 'Anyone else scared of the Devil's Hound?'

Hari stood up. 'Not me. But my animals are scared of something, that's for sure. It's probably just the weather…'

'So come.'

'Lizzie, I can't leave them. They're too jumpy. They need me.'

Whenever the circus had to move on, there was always a moment when the main pole of the big top was dropped. For an instant the tent walls would billow out as the roof fell in, then the whole grand affair would crumple to the ground, the air rushing out of it. Lizzie felt just like that now as she let out a long sigh.

'Is *anyone* going to join me?' she said. 'I ain't going to twist your arms. I'll go alone if I 'ave to.'

'What do you reckon, Dru?' said Malachy. 'We can't

let the young lady go exploring a spooky graveyard all on her lonesome, can we?'

'That would not be *gallant* of us, I fear,' Dru said, shaking his head in mock sadness.

'It seems we are in agreement, me old china.'

'It seems we are, *mon camerade*.' Dru and Malachy solemnly shook hands, and Lizzie had to laugh at their tomfoolery.

Malachy tossed his walking stick from one hand to the other. 'I'd better bring this. The ground might be uneven, and you never know when someone might need a whack on the bonce.'

'Does your dad know you talk like that?' Erin challenged him.

Malachy's eyes flashed. 'No, and you ain't going to tell him, Erin Sullivan. That goes for all of us. We're a gang, right? So we keep schtum about what we get up to.'

'Unless it's an emergency,' Lizzie added.

'Well, yeah,' admitted Malachy. 'Obviously not then.'

'Please don't go!' Nora begged them. 'I know you think it's all a big adventure, but what if something terrible happens to you? The Devil's Hound is *real*,

I *know* it is!'

'What's going to happen to us?' Malachy scoffed. 'I don't remember nothing in the Bible about the Devil having a hound!'

'There's other books than the Bible,' Erin said darkly. Nora nudged her to shut up.

Malachy took Lizzie's arm and they walked out of the tent together. 'There's nothing up there but a lot of dead people, and the dead can't hurt the living, can they?'

'Just be careful,' Nora called out after them. 'Promise?'

'I promise,' Lizzie said, smiling over her shoulder.

'Heck of a big moon tonight,' Lizzie said, glancing up at the sky. 'We won't even need a lantern.'

Dru looked up and down the road, which looked as dark as an undertaker's hat, even beneath the bright full moon. '*C'est très romantique,*' he sighed. 'A moonlight stroll through the beautiful English countryside.'

'Leave it out!' laughed Lizzie.

'I worry about you sometimes, Dru,' Malachy said.

His footsteps crunched on the gravelly road. 'You don't seem right in the head.'

'What can I say?' said Dru. 'We French speak as we feel.'

They kept up the playful chatter as they walked up the road towards the cemetery. Even though nobody said so, Lizzie knew that they were all talking to keep the silence at bay. If they stopped, the quiet would creep back in, and they wouldn't feel so brave.

As they continued down the lonely road, Lizzie grew more and more aware of the sounds around her. Her own breathing began to sound sinister, her own footsteps sounded like they belonged to someone else.

Lizzie wondered as she walked: was Malachy right? The dead couldn't harm the living, could they?

Of course they couldn't. Besides, she didn't believe in ghosts.

Then she remembered. She'd talked with a dead man that very day. Becky's father.

Ghosts are real, she thought to herself. *I have to believe in them now. Whether we can see them or not, we won't be alone in that cemetery. The spirits of the dead will be all around us.*

Lizzie thought about Becky's father. He'd only been

dead for two days, so he didn't look bad. But what about the old ones?

Crunch, crunch, crunch went their feet on the pathway. The walls of Kensal Green Cemetery were up ahead.

There were bodies in the ground that had been dead for years, long since decayed to rags and bones. Would their ghosts have skulls for faces and outstretched skeleton arms? Would they be invisible, or look like a shroud floating in the air?

A horrible feeling struck her.

What if I see them?

'You're very quiet all of a sudden, Lizzie,' Malachy said.

'I'm fine,' she said hastily. 'Just thinking.'

They reached the huge ornamental gates through which the funeral procession had passed. Beyond, Lizzie could see winding paths and dark vegetation, with neat rows of graves laid out. A stout iron chain had been wound around the bars and the padlock that fastened it looked heavy as a ship's anchor.

'Should have expected that, really,' Malachy said. He tested the padlock, which was locked fast.

Lizzie looked up at the spikes topping the gate.

'I don't fancy going over that. I'd be skewered. Should we turn back?'

'Give up that easy? Never. Allow me.' Dru sidled along to a section of wall. It was higher than the top of his head, but Lizzie knew Dru could climb it with ease. Sure enough, he took a few steps back and then ran at it. A powerful leap, a scuff of boot on the masonry, and next second his outflung hands caught the top of the wall. He dangled for a moment, then pulled himself up using just the strength in his arms. A few swinging kicks brought his legs up, and then he was straddling the wall, smiling down at them.

'Good view from up there?' Lizzie teased.

'*Très belle!* Malachy, pass me up your stick, *s'il vous plaît.* It's a little lonely up on this wall all by myself. I think you should join me.'

Lizzie let Malachy go first. By grabbing the outstretched stick, he was able to clamber his way up. His club foot made the climb difficult, but Lizzie knew better than to offer him a hand. He never let it get in the way of doing what he wanted to do. An offer of help would have been insulting – and unnecessary.

'Up you come, slowcoach,' Malachy called to her. A few moments of scrambling later, the three of them were sitting looking over the cemetery like owls brooding on a rafter.

Lizzie thought of Nora and Erin, snug in their bunks by now, and wondered if they were lying awake worrying about her. If they could see what she was seeing, they wouldn't sleep a wink, that was for sure.

Vast stone monuments rose out of the earth: angels with blank eyes and sorrowful faces, holding skulls in their hands; mournful shrouded figures looming over the graves; indistinct shapes casting deformed shadows in the moonlight. The headstones looked white as exposed bones. A little mist was creeping through the trees, veiling the ground in a gauzy shroud. *It's just like my vision*, Lizzie thought with a shudder.

'Brrr,' Malachy said. 'Chilly out here, isn't it?' He rubbed his arms, which were covered in gooseflesh.

'We'd better go down,' Lizzie said. 'Everyone ready?'

They hesitated for a moment. Once they dropped down onto the ground on the other side of the wall, there would be no easy way out. They'd be trapped in there with anything else that might be roaming around the graveyard.

Lizzie took a deep breath, lowered herself down until she was hanging by her hands, then dropped the rest of the way.

Dru and Malachy followed, not saying a word.

Slowly, one cautious step at a time, they explored the cemetery. Instead of keeping to the paths, where they might have been seen, they moved between the burial plots. Lizzie had to fight the urge to whisper 'Sorry!' every time she stepped over one of the graves.

'What are we looking for?' whispered Malachy.

'We'll know when we find it,' Lizzie assured him.

Warily Lizzie approached a huge tomb with marble wreaths on all four corners. It wasn't the sort of tomb that only held one person. There would be a whole family in there, stacked on the shelves in their coffins. Lizzie's breath caught in her throat as she saw a hooded form beyond the tomb, waiting silently in the moonlight.

Then she relaxed again. It was only another carved angel, its hands covering its face.

'Here's a fresh one,' Malachy said, beckoning her over. It was a humble grave, nothing more than a mound of recently dug earth with a simple wooden cross as its marker. Somehow it didn't seem as threatening as the rest of the cemetery. It felt peaceful, though sad.

Lizzie read the painted letters on the cross. 'Jacob Hayward, Farmer of this Parish…' She felt cold as she saw the date of his death. It was three days ago.

This is Becky's father's grave.

She touched the horse brass in her pocket, then quickly pulled her hand away. She had to do something before she left, but what?

While the others searched, she picked a small posy of the hedgerow flowers that were growing wild nearby and laid it on top of the grave. 'There you go, sir. Rest in peace. Becky sends her love.'

As she walked away, she realized she was on her own. There was no sign of Dru and Malachy. She listened for the sound of Malachy's stick, but the only noise was the rustling of leaves.

'Dru?' She headed onto the path, beside a tall black headstone. 'Mal?'

From somewhere close by came a scratching sound, like long nails dragged across wood. It was the sound someone would make if they were trying to scrape their way out of a coffin. Had someone been buried alive? Lizzie felt her heart thumping painfully behind her ribcage.

She approached a low tomb. There it was again –

skritch-scratch.

'H-hello?'

Something leaped up from behind the tomb, all pale face and grasping hands. Lizzie shrieked as it came for her.

'Boo!' it said, and burst out laughing.

Lizzie clenched her fists, panting in shock. 'Don't do that, Dru! God, you nearly gave me a heart attack!'

'You should have seen the look on your face,' Dru chuckled. Then he fell over into a shrub as Lizzie gave him a shove from behind.

He picked his way out, shaking leaves from his hair. 'OK. I deserved that.'

'Yes, you did. Bloomin' idiot.'

They heard the tap-scrape, tap-scrape, of Malachy coming closer. 'Nothing over here,' he called softly to them. 'Just graves, moths and a bat or two.'

'Then I guess we can leave,' Dru said, shrugging. 'Have you seen enough now, Lizzie?'

Lizzie froze. Malachy was standing still looking at her. So why could she still hear the scrape of his club foot on the gravel?

'Listen!' she hissed.

Moments passed. They could all hear it now. *Scrape.*

Rattle. Scrape.

Malachy listened carefully, then turned in a new direction. He motioned for them to follow. The noise grew louder as they came closer to whatever was making it.

'Sounds like digging,' Lizzie whispered.

'*Exactement,*' said Dru.

'Digging a new grave, maybe?'

'In the middle of the night?' Malachy sucked at his teeth. 'Unlikely. Everyone, get down. We'll hide behind this tomb.'

They all pressed themselves up against the cold marble and moved as close as they dared. The sound of digging was very close. They must be right on top of it now. From behind the tomb, a ghostly light was flickering.

Lizzie peered around the corner. By the feeble light of a shuttered lantern dangling from an angel's hand, she saw two shadowy figures. Were they even human? She strained to see closer.

From the bushes, something howled. It moved. Lizzie glimpsed dark fur, a flash of yellowish eyes, the glint of snarling teeth.

She couldn't move. Sheer terror had locked every

muscle in her body.

The thing loped out in front of the lantern, and a massive shadow loomed before her. If it was a dog, and not some kind of wolf, it was the largest one she'd ever seen. It was something from prehistoric times, a hideous memory surging back to life. It howled again.

Then it turned its head toward her, bared its teeth, and crouched ready to spring.

Much too late, Lizzie knew it was real. The thing that haunted the cemetery, the beast Erin and Nora had tried to warn her about...

The Devil's Hound!

CHAPTER 8

Dru grabbed her hand. 'Lizzie, *run*!'

She ran. Together they sprinted through the cemetery, leaping over the graves and ducking tree branches. Lizzie glanced back to see if Malachy was following, and saw him hobbling along as fast as he could, gasping as he struggled to get away from the beast at the graveside.

Behind him, the monstrous dog emerged from the shadows. It howled again. *That's three times*, Lizzie thought. *If Ma Sullivan's right, it'll come for my soul.*

'We should never have come 'ere!' she cried, clinging tight to Dru's hand. 'There's things here we oughtn't to have stirred up!'

'Save your breath for running!'

They ran alongside a long cypress hedge, past marble monuments and urns on pedestals. For a moment, Lizzie thought they'd escaped the hound. But then, from behind, came the sound of a long rattling snarl and three sharp barks.

She didn't dare to look round again. She just ran for her life.

'This way!' Dru pulled her to the left and then they were running downhill, past the low burial plots they'd seen before. Lizzie's chest ached and her throat was raw from the chill night air.

'There's the gates,' said Dru. 'That's where we came in. We're nearly out!'

The hound barked again, much closer this time. It was coming for them. Heavy paws pounded on the gravel path.

'Keep running!' Malachy yelled from behind. 'Don't stop!'

Dru let go of Lizzie's hand. He put on a burst of speed and ran towards the wall, like an athelete approaching a high jump. A single leap, and he caught hold of the top of the wall with both hands. He hauled himself up with the strength of his arms until he was able to swing a leg over the top and sit securely.

He reached out. 'Lizzie, jump! I'll catch you.'

'I bloomin' 'ope so,' Lizzie gasped. The downhill sprint meant she was half running, half falling. She tried to speed up as Dru had done, thinking she'd launch herself at the wall. But her legs were suddenly a confused jumble, and the next thing she knew, she'd tripped over a pot of roses someone had left on a grave.

She stumbled and fell forwards. Her arms came down on sharp gravel, her knee on the rough ground. She tried to stop but she was rolling over and over, helpless as a rag doll. The moon flashed past her eyes again and again as she tumbled down the hill.

Stunned and dizzy, she struggled back to her feet. She'd landed at the foot of the wall. Where was Malachy? She turned around to look – and there was the hound, only feet away, all teeth and bristling fur, coming at her nightmarishly fast. It leaped, gaping jaws lunging at her throat.

She screamed. In that moment of cold terror, she suddenly understood why the scream she'd heard in her vision had sounded so familiar. A girl's voice, screaming as if she was being murdered…

I heard myself scream, she thought. *It was me dying.*

She could feel the thing's hot breath on her face.

Next second, the dog's snarl turned into a startled yelp. Something whacked it from the side. 'Get away, you brute!' yelled a familiar voice. 'Garn, get out of it!'

'Malachy?'

Brandishing his stick in both hands, Malachy charged at the hound. 'Bad dog!'

It scrabbled away from him, turned and snarled, crouching low on its front paws. Malachy swung his stick in a wide arc, keeping it at bay.

From somewhere in the distance came the shouts of angry men. A lantern was swinging through the trees up on the crest of the hill.

'Lizzie, get up here, quick!' Dru was holding his hand out.

Lizzie grabbed hold of it and scrambled up the wall, with Dru helping her up. She almost jumped down the other side, before it struck her that Malachy might still need help.

Malachy backed towards the wall, jabbing his stick at the snarling dog. He glanced up at Dru. 'You ready?'

'Come on!' yelled Dru.

Malachy shoved the stick upwards. As the dog came

bounding towards him, Dru caught hold of it and pulled. Lizzie threw her arms around Dru's waist, keeping him securely on top of the wall, while Dru pulled Malachy all the way up to their level.

The dog's snapping jaws caught Malachy's boot. He kicked hard, but the teeth sank deep into the leather and locked like a vice. Lizzie and Dru heaved with all their strength.

'Get off me!' Malachy shrieked.

The lantern swung to point in their direction. Lizzie heard gruff voices shouting, and whoever was holding it began to run.

Suddenly Malachy's boot came off. He came free with such force the three of them almost fell off the wall. 'Whoa!'

'I'm OK,' Malachy panted, settling down between them. Lizzie patted him on the back, feeling grateful for his bravery.

Down below, the dog tore and ripped at the boot, pulling it to pieces.

'I think we're about to have company,' Malachy said, glancing at the approaching figures. 'Should we wait and see who it is?'

'I've had enough nasty surprises for one night,'

Lizzie said. 'Let's go.'

They hurried back along the road, with Malachy moving even slower than usual thanks to his bootless good foot. From behind the cemetery wall came a long, mournful howl. They picked up their pace, keen to put as much distance between them and the Devil's Hound as they could.

'There's a light in the tea tent,' Malachy pointed out as they drew near to the circus once again. 'What's Ma Sullivan doing up at this hour?'

'Let's go see. I could murder a cup of cocoa.' Lizzie rubbed her hands together.

But it wasn't Ma Sullivan who was waiting for them. It was Nora, Erin and Hari, huddled around three cups of steaming tea, playing cards by the light of an oil lantern. Nora sprang up and hugged Lizzie as she saw her come in. 'Oh, thank God. You're safe.'

'None of us could sleep, so we decided to wait up for you,' Hari said.

'We heard howling,' Erin said, 'and Nora thought you were dead for sure.'

Nora pushed her. 'You thought so too, Erin.'

'She was crying like a baby—' Erin saw the look on Lizzie's face. 'What happened? You look like death!'

Malachy sat down. 'Get us a brew. I'll tell you all about it.'

So Malachy explained everything that had happened, while the others listened like wide-eyed children being told a ghost story around a fire.

Lizzie sat next to Dru, thinking about how easily he'd lifted her up the wall. The boy was so much stronger than he looked. As she sipped the tea Nora brought her, warmth seeped back into her bones. The nightmare chase in the cemetery seemed almost unreal now, like a half-remembered dream.

When Malachy had finished, Nora shook her head. 'Oh, Lizzie, why didn't you listen? It's not all nonsense, you know, the old stories. You almost fell foul of the Devil's Hound.'

Lizzie shuddered. 'It was huge. Teeth like broken glass.'

'Just like our ma told you,' Erin said. 'Maybe next time we tell you not to risk your neck going up into that cemetery, you'll listen. There's the Devil's business going on up there. It's not for the likes of us to go messing with.'

'It's a bad business, all right,' said Malachy, leaning back in his chair. 'But it ain't the Devil up there, and it weren't his hound that tore my boot off.'

'Oh, was it not?' Nora seemed exasperated. 'And I suppose you've got it all worked out, have you?'

'Might have.' Malachy scratched his chin.

'Well?'

'I think we ran across a couple of graverobbers,' Malachy said, in a matter-of-fact tone.

Lizzie was about to laugh the idea off, but stopped short. The sounds of digging, the mysterious figures, the lantern, the guard dog … Malachy's theory made sense. They all stared at each other as the horror of the idea sank in.

Only one thing didn't add up for her. 'Why would anyone want to steal a dead body?'

'Witchcraft,' said Erin. 'There's things a witch can do with a dead man's skin, if you get it off all in one piece—'

'It's not the corpse they want,' Malachy interrupted her. 'They often bury rich people with their jewellery. Sometimes it's just because old people's knuckles swell up and the undertaker can't get their rings off. But some greedy old toffs can't bear the idea of giving their wealth to anyone else, so they try and take it with 'em.'

Lizzie gasped. 'That toff funeral we saw when we arrived here!'

'Exactly.'

Hari frowned. 'If the undertaker can't get the rings off, how do graverobbers do it?'

'Trust me, mate, you really don't want to know.'

Lizzie's stomach churned at the thought. 'They've got to be stopped,' she said. 'It ain't fair on the dead people. What's it say on the graves? "Rest in peace". So how can they rest peacefully if people are digging them up and stealing their things?'

She thought of Becky's father and the humble grave she'd seen. She still had the horse brass in her pocket that was the pair of the one he'd been buried with. On impulse, she reached in and touched it. Maybe Jacob Hayward could help. After all, who better to tell her what was going on at the cemetery than one of the dead people?

Instantly the tea tent and everyone in it vanished from around her. She was plunged into a vision so powerful that it completely drowned out the real world. Swirling black clouds bloomed around her, like ink in water.

In front of her was Becky's father's disembodied face.

And he was screaming: '*Sacred ground! It was sacred ground! They had no right!*'

The voice echoed, as if he was yelling from the end of a long tunnel. For the first time, Lizzie felt frightened of him. This angry ghost couldn't be more different from the peaceful spirit she'd seen before.

'*Thieves! They had no right!*'

'What do you mean?' Lizzie tried to ask, but her breath wouldn't come.

As suddenly as the vision had started, it ended, and Lizzie was back in her chair with a jolt. The others surrounded her, looking on with anxious faces.

'Lizzie, what happened?' Malachy said. 'Your eyes were all white. Like you were having a fit.'

'Should we take you to the doctor?' Erin felt Lizzie's forehead.

She coughed. 'I had a vision. I saw Becky's father. He spoke to me.'

Erin jerked her hand away as if it had been burned. 'Her *dead* father?'

'Obviously her dead father! She don't have any other fathers, does she? He was really upset. Screaming.'

'What did he say?' asked Hari.

'He was yelling about thieves, and how it was sacred ground, and they had no right. I think Malachy's sussed it. There's graverobbers at the cemetery, and they've stolen something from him. Disturbed his rest.'

Malachy drained the last of his tea and wiped his mouth with his sleeve. 'There's only one thing for it, then. We have to go back tomorrow night to see if Lizzie's right.'

'And if I am?'

'Then we'll catch these graverobbers before they can strike again!'

CHAPTER 9

'Mornin', treacle!' called Anita, the circus dwarf, from the door of her trailer. 'Ain't you meant to be off to the doctor's with all the rest?'

Lizzie yawned and stretched. For a moment, she was confused. She wasn't ill – why would she need to see the doctor? Then suddenly she remembered: it was vaccination day. 'What time is it?' Lizzie asked, climbing out of her bed and throwing on some clothes.

'Time you was in the show tent, my girl. That's where the others are meeting before setting off for the doctor's house. Hey, you're not worried about the jab, are yer? Don't be. It's over in a jiff.'

'I'm trying not to think about the jab. I'm just looking forward to visiting JoJo.'

'Good girl. 'Ere, pop inside a moment. I've got something for you to give him.' It was a little tin, tied with a bright golden bow. 'Peppermint creams,' Anita explained. 'He loves 'em. And if the doctor says he can't have 'em yet, then stick 'em by his bed for when he's better.'

Mario, the circus giant, stopped Lizzie on her way out. 'You taking those up to JoJo? Can you give him this from me, too?'

'A book?' The cover read *The Life and Opinions of Tristram Shandy, Gentleman.*

'It's the funniest thing I ever read,' said Mario. 'I don't want JoJo getting gloomy up there by himself. That wouldn't be right.'

'I agree,' said Lizzie with a firm nod. *Nothing's worse than a sad clown*, she thought.

As she turned to go, she saw the Amazon Queen and Dru's father, Pierre, coming towards her. Both of them were carrying little bundles.

'Are those for JoJo, by any chance?' she asked with a grin.

By the time she reached the show tent, she'd been

given so many presents for the sick clown that Hari had to find her a spare hessian sack to carry them all in.

'I feel like ruddy Father Christmas!' she laughed. 'Everyone loves JoJo, don't they?'

'All one big family at Fitzy's,' Hari said, quoting one of the ringmaster's favourite sayings.

It was true, though, Lizzie thought. JoJo's blood relations were all far away in Newcastle, but he wasn't alone. Everyone in the extended family of the circus was rallying around to help him. She felt proud to be a part of it as she hefted the heavy sack onto her shoulder and started walking with the others, down the country lane to Doctor Gladwell's house.

Doctor Gladwell welcomed the small crowd of circus people into his parlour. 'Now, you may have heard a whole load of silly nonsense about the evils of vaccination,' he began, 'but it's a perfectly harmless process. All we do is give you a dose of weak germs, so your body learns how to fight the strong germs of smallpox.'

'Do you have to use a needle?' asked Collette. She

looked pale and faint.

'I'm afraid so, young lady. The vaccine has to go into your blood, so – pop!'

Collette clutched at her brother's arm. 'Dru, *je vais vomir.*'

Malachy strolled up to the doctor and tugged his sleeve up. 'Go on, Doc. You can do me first.'

'Brave lad. Well done.'

Lizzie was impressed, and more so when the syringe came out. Malachy's bold smile didn't even flicker. The syringe looked like a miniature brass cannon with a needle like a giant insect's sting.

It took only a few seconds. 'There! All done.' Doctor Gladwell cleaned the needle, then patted Malachy on the back. 'Off you go. Now, Lizzie?' Lizzie flinched when the needle went in. Collette rolled her eyes and sank into a chair, her hand pressed to her forehead. *What a drama queen,* Lizzie thought.

'Splendid,' said the doctor. 'Brave souls all.'

'Can we visit JoJo now, please?' Lizzie immediately asked.

'I'm afraid he's asleep,' said the doctor. 'Now, who's next?'

Lizzie and Malachy glanced at one another. While

the doctor's back was turned, they slipped out into the hallway.

'He didn't say *no*, did he?' Lizzie whispered.

'Let's give JoJo the presents anyway,' said Malachy. 'It'll be nice for him to wake up to, won't it? Seeing all that stuff.'

'So where is he?'

Malachy peered upstairs. 'Probably in one of the bedrooms.'

They crept upstairs, feeling like thieves. The hallway smelled of beeswax, from the candles and the polish, and a strange chemical smell too. It turned Lizzie's stomach. 'What's that pong?'

'I dunno. Carbolic soap, I think.'

It's not carbolic, Lizzie thought. *I've smelled carbolic a thousand times, when Pa was making fake sores on his arms and legs with soap and ash. It's something worse.* But she said nothing.

The upstairs hallway lay before them, with doors all along it. One had a trolley outside, with a white enamel basin and a jug of water on it. Another syringe, every bit as fearsome as the one the doctor had used on Malachy, rested in the basin. There was blood on its tip.

'This must be his room.' Gently, so as not to wake him, Lizzie pushed open the door. To her surprise, a low moan came from inside.

'JoJo? Oh, *no*!'

The clown was barely recognizable. Weeping sores covered his face. Lizzie's horror only grew when she saw there were white lumps on his tongue. She dumped the sack of presents on a sideboard and ran to his bedside.

'How could he be so much worse?' Malachy said, shocked.

'They're murderin' me,' JoJo groaned. 'Stabbing me all over like … Julius Caesar.'

'He's not making any sense,' Lizzie said. 'JoJo, it's us! Lizzie and Malachy! Can you hear me?'

'Lizzie?' JoJo's eyes opened wide. He looked terrified. 'She mustn't come here. Tell her to stay away.'

'I *am* Lizzie.' She wanted to cry. 'Your friend.'

'They're trying to kill me with their needles!' JoJo spluttered, then fell backwards against the pillow. He looked dead. But just as Lizzie was about to shake him, he heaved a huge rattling breath.

'What are you doing in here? Get out!'

Mrs Crowe stood in the doorway, syringe in her hand. She was grasping it like a dagger.

'What's happened to him?' Lizzie demanded.

'The patient is delirious. He needs to rest, or he'll never recover.'

'But we—'

'Out!' She flung out a branch-like arm, pointing them back down the stairs.

Lizzie waited until they were safely out of the house before saying anything. 'I don't trust that old woman,' she muttered. 'She's a nasty piece of work.'

'She's trying to help JoJo get better, though,' Malachy said, but he didn't sound too certain.

'That's as may be. Still, I wish someone else was helping look after him. Someone kind like Doctor Gladwell, instead of that crabby old cow. I don't trust her.'

As the circus people began to filter out of the house, fresh bandages on their arms, Malachy casually took Lizzie aside. 'Fancy a stroll down the towpath?'

'Don't mind if I do,' she said, knowing exactly why he'd offered. They needed to make a plan.

'See you back at the site!' Malachy waved to the

others, as he and Lizzie headed for the Grand Union Canal. Once they were out of earshot, Malachy said, 'We have to catch those graverobbers red-handed.'

'Shouldn't we get proof first? I mean, we don't know if it *is* graverobbers yet. Not for certain.'

'What proof do you want? Open graves? Dead people with no jewellery?'

Lizzie thought. 'I left some flowers on Becky's father's grave. If those flowers aren't there tonight, it means someone's been and dug it up.'

'That's only one grave!' Malachy said, with a disbelieving laugh. 'What about all the thousands of others?'

'That's the one we need to check.'

'Why?'

'Because his spirit's not at rest.'

Malachy shuddered. 'I forgot you're talking to ghosts now. Remind me not to laugh at Ma Sullivan again.'

Lizzie peered into the distance. Two men dressed in the rough overcoats and heavy boots of canal workers were standing by the waterside. They looked alike enough to be brothers, though one was clearly older.

At first Lizzie thought someone had fallen in, because a shape was slowly sinking out of sight below the water, but then she realized the men weren't helping. Lizzie noted how one of them was keeping lookout while the other one fumbled with a sack.

'Do those two look suspicious to you?' she asked Malachy.

'Very,' Malachy agreed.

Lizzie slowed down.

'No, don't stop, keep walking!' Malachy hissed. 'Pretend we haven't noticed them.'

The man with the sack, the older of the two, held it over the canal and shook it out. A few articles of clothing fell in. Clearly they weren't sinking quickly enough for his satisfaction, because he sat down on the side and poked them under with his foot.

The lookout noticed them approaching. He nudged his companion, who turned to look, then hastily put the sack behind his back. The lookout folded his arms and glared at them. *We're just two kids walking by a canal,* Lizzie thought. *What are you going to do, eh?*

Then the man with the sack quickly fished a bright metallic object out of it and threw it in. It caught the sun as it sank, making a warm flash of gold.

'Did you see what that was?' Malachy whispered.

Lizzie stared at the ripples. She was almost

positive that it was a horse brass. *In fact,* she thought, *I'd swear to it.*

They were only yards away from the two men now. Both men stood their ground, blocking the towpath. The younger had his arms folded across his chest, while the older man slowly rolled up his sleeves to reveal thick hairy arms.

'Morning,' Lizzie said.

They didn't reply.

'What are you doing?' she persisted.

'Mindin' our own business,' said the younger one. 'Why don't you do the same?'

'Shove off,' added the other.

Lizzie wasn't having that. 'I saw you. You were chucking things in the canal. What were you doing that for?'

'That's for me to know and you to wonder about, you snotty-nosed little brat,' sneered the lookout. 'You keep asking questions, you'll feel the back of my hand.'

'That's no way to speak to a lady,' Malachy said. 'You need a lesson in manners.'

'Lady!' Both men laughed. 'That ain't no lady. Your girl's a grubby little ragamuffin, mate.'

'She's not my girl. And you take that back, right

now.' Malachy's fingers tightened on his stick. He was white with anger. Lizzie knew, in that moment, that Malachy would attack both of them without any care for his own safety.

'That was a horse brass you threw in the canal, wasn't it?' Lizzie pushed up to the man who had the sack, to show him she wasn't afraid.

'I don't have to tell you nothing!'

'Where did you get it?'

'Come on,' the lookout said. 'These two are trouble.' He tugged his companion's arm and tried to leave.

'Oh no you don't!' Lizzie saw the sack wasn't quite empty. 'Open up that sack. Show us what's in it.'

'Not likely. I said, come *on*!'

'Give it here!' Lizzie yelled, grabbing hold of the sack with both hands.

The man ripped the sack away and gave her a brutal shove. Lizzie staggered back a few steps. Her arms windmilled for a second as she struggled to regain her balance, then she fell backwards and the freezing cold water of the Grand Union canal engulfed her.

Everything was muffled and echoey under the water. She heard Malachy screaming her name, but it sounded like the distant tolling of a bell. She gasped, but instead of air, a mouthful of filthy canal water filled her mouth.

I'm going to drown.

Panic siezed her. Gagging, choking, she kicked and flailed her arms. Children from Rat's Castle didn't learn how to swim, and Lizzie was no exception. By sheer good fortune, her head broke the water and she managed to draw a lungful of air. Malachy was there, holding out his stick, yelling for her to grab hold of it.

Even as she floundered, Lizzie knew she had to keep track of the two men. She saw them running away down the towpath, the sack bouncing on the man's shoulder.

She tried to yell to Malachy, but started to sink again. Stinking green water washed into her mouth and nose. Before she could stop herself, she'd breathed it in and felt herself going under…

CHAPTER 10

Lizzie's clothes billowed around her as she sank. Her feet brushed the bottom. The water wasn't deep, but it was deep enough to drown in.

Something hard prodded her in the ribs. Her mind flashed back to the man poking the clothes under the surface with his foot. *He's trying to drown me!*

She grabbed at it, thinking she'd drag him down with her, but her hands closed on a wooden pole. As her last breath bubbled up around her and her mind sank into roaring blackness, she felt the pole lift.

Suddenly, she was breathing air again. She coughed foul water from her lungs and clung onto the pole.

Her vision cleared enough for her to see Malachy gripping the other end of the pole, pulling her towards the towpath.

He grabbed her by the shoulder and hauled her, limp as a half-drowned kitten, out of the murky water. She doubled over on the stones and half coughed, half spewed what felt like a gallon of liquid. Red fireworks were going off behind her eyes.

'I thought I'd lost you!' Malachy walloped her on the back, trying to drive the water out of her lungs.

After the fourth or fifth smack, Lizzie begged him to stop. 'You're going to break me spine,' she gasped.

'We need to get you somewhere warm and dry. You're shivering!'

Lizzie was freezing, but she barely even noticed. She was trembling from shock, not from the cold. Those men hadn't pushed her in as a prank or out of spite. They had been trying to kill her!

'What ha-happened to those two blokes?'

'They legged it,' Malachy said, making a sour face. 'Lucky for us they did. Or they might have tried to finish both of us off.'

Lizzie glanced back at the canal, desperate to know what they'd been throwing in there. 'I'm sure that was a horse brass they threw in. We could fish around, see what's down there...'

Malachy pulled her away. 'Oh no you don't. You are *not* going back in that water. I'm taking you back to the circus.'

'No. Let's go to Becky's farm. It's closer. And there's some things she needs to know.'

Dressed in some spare dry clothes of Becky's, Lizzie huddled by the fire, grateful for its warmth. She could still taste the canal water every time she sniffed.

Becky looked much happier than she had been when Lizzie first met her. The farmhouse was tidy, with fresh flowers on the table. Obviously, the message from her dead father had put her mind at ease.

'Becky ... there's something I've got to tell you.' Lizzie had to get it out quick, before she lost her nerve. 'Your pa spoke to me again.'

'Really?' Becky looked delighted, but when she saw Lizzie's solemn face, her smile vanished. 'What's wrong? He's not upset with me, is he? I've worked so hard—'

'No! It's nothing like that. I think he might

not be at peace.'

'I don't understand.'

'Better start at the beginning, Lizzie,' said Malachy. 'We went up to the cemetery to investigate. There were two men there. We think they were digging.'

Malachy told the whole story, right up to the part when they escaped. Then Lizzie took over.

'As soon as I touched the horse brass, I saw your father. He was so upset – he kept shouting "Thieves!"'

'You think someone's robbed my father's grave?' Becky's unbelieving sob was horrible to hear. 'But why? He was poor. He didn't have any jewels, only Dandy's other brass!'

As she watched her friend's face crumple in tears in an all too familiar way, Lizzie decided she was going to bring the graverobbers to justice, no matter what.

'I don't know,' she said. 'I can't make sense of it. Perhaps they mistook his grave for someone else's?' *That could explain why the men were throwing the things into the canal*, Lizzie thought. In the dark of the cemetery they thought they'd found gold, but it had turned out to be just a horse brass.

'There's something else, isn't there?' Becky whispered. 'What aren't you telling me?'

Lizzie sighed. 'The two men who pushed me into the canal? I'd swear they were the same two men from the cemetery. They were throwing things in the water. Clothes, and something that looked like…'

'Like what?' Becky grasped her hands.

She had to say it. 'Like a horse brass. I'm so sorry.'

Becky closed her eyes. Fresh tears rolled down her face. Then she stood up and quietly crossed over to the window, where she stood looking out at the farm for a long while.

Lizzie sat in silence, wondering if she'd done the right thing. Maybe it would have been kinder not to tell Becky the truth. She would have been none the wiser.

'Thank you,' Becky said. She turned round. Her eyes were red, but the tears were gone. 'My father fought for this farm, did I tell you that? They tried to force him to sell it when I was a baby. The canal people wanted the land. But he held his ground, for my mum's sake, and for mine. I think I've cried enough, don't you? I think it's time I started fighting.'

'We're going to the cemetery again tonight,' Lizzie said. 'If we find anything, I'll come straight over and tell you.'

'You won't have to,' Becky said. 'I'm coming with you.'

'You are?' Malachy boggled.

'Just try and stop me.' Becky glanced up at the shotgun that hung over the fireplace. 'If some gang of graverobbing low-lifes really has disturbed my father's rest, then they're going to pay. I'm going to help catch them.'

'Let's all meet up in Lizzie's caravan after tonight's show.' Malachy sprang to his feet. 'Speaking of which, we need to get back. You're performing tonight.'

'Oh, lord, don't remind me.' The thought of embarrassing herself on horseback again filled Lizzie with dread.

Lizzie walked back to the circus with Malachy, step by reluctant step. If only there was some way she could get out of her commitment. She considered telling Fitzy about her brush with drowning, but decided against it. The showman had enough on his mind already, and she'd given her word that she'd perform.

'Penny for your thoughts?' Malachy eventually said.

'I wish I could wave a magic wand and make Erin's wrist better,' she said. 'All those people looking at me – I can't stand it.'

'You'll be fine.'

'But I won't, Mal! I won't! I can't do the routine, and it's no good pretending I can. I'd be better off as a clown than an equestrian. I should have taken JoJo's part, not Erin's!'

'Hmm,' said Malachy.

'What?' Lizzie was instantly suspicious. 'I know that face.'

'What face?'

'You're scheming.'

'Never mind,' Malachy said breezily. 'It was just an idea.'

'What idea?'

'It doesn't matter.'

Lizzie said half-seriously, 'Do you want to get pushed in the canal too? Spit it out!'

'All right!' Malachy laughed. 'Maybe, instead of trying to do Erin's routine the way she does it, you should mess it up on purpose? Play it for laughs. Then Nora can do the tricks properly.'

Lizzie thought about it. 'It's worth a try. I dunno if I

like the idea of being laughed at, though.'

'And another thing. Since you're talking to dead people now, why don't you do seances?'

'Seances?' Lizzie repeated.

'You know – shows where you contact spirits. They're all the rage in London society. It's in the papers.'

'What, for money?'

'You could make a mint.' Malachy winked. 'I'm sure my pop would be happy. Imagine if you could comfort more of the Beckys of this world, and make a few bob doing it!'

'I dunno.' Lizzie kicked a loose stone into the canal. 'It don't feel right to me, making money out of people's grief.'

'It doesn't stop undertakers, does it? If nobody died, they'd be out of a job.'

Lizzie silently forgave Malachy for being so pushy. She knew he was worried about his father's debt problems. Besides, he was probably right. People would pay handsomely for messages from beyond the grave. But she knew, in her heart, it wasn't something she should profit from. Her powers were for doing good in the world, not for making money.

I bet people would pay anything to see their loved ones

again, she thought. *I know I would. If I could just see my ma again, or my brother…*

Then it suddenly flashed upon her, a thought so simple and so powerful it stopped her in her tracks.

Maybe I can!

CHAPTER 11

Back in her trailer, Lizzie quickly changed into her mystic robes. Even with tonight's performance to come, and the graveyard trip after that, she still had to put in her shift as the circus fortune-teller. 'You're the Magnificent Lizzie Brown,' Fitzy had reminded her more than once. 'People come a long way to see you.'

But the idea she'd had was still preying on her mind. She rummaged through her few possessions, looking for the most precious treasure of them all. It had to be here. It couldn't have been lost.

Of course – she'd left it under her pillow. There it was, a decorative tortoiseshell comb, missing a tooth.

As Lizzie held it now, she remembered her mother putting her hair up with it, singing softly to her all the while:

'I dream of Jeannie with the light brown hair,

Borne like a vapour on the summer air.'

The comb, and those memories, were all she had left of her. Lizzie was lucky it had been in her hair when she'd fled Rat's Castle. She'd left all her other possessions, few though they were, behind.

Her shift was about to start. Lizzie ran to the fortune telling tent, praying no customers were waiting for her. To her delight, there was nobody there. She had a few moments to herself.

She sat quietly, holding her mother's comb just like she'd held the horse brass. Part of her was worried that it wouldn't work … and part was worried that it would. What if her mother wasn't at peace? Maybe it would be better not to find out.

Nothing happened. Doubts swirled in her mind. She'd had the comb for years now, so maybe it didn't count as her mother's any more. She stroked the comb, remembering she'd done that with the brass.

Still nothing happened.

Perhaps it had just been a fluke that she'd been able

to 'see' Becky's father. Or worse, what if her mother had forgotten about her? She was up in Heaven, after all. Why should she care about her daughter stuck down here on earth?

'*I will never forget you, Lizzie.*'

It was her mother's voice, strong, clear and calm.

Lizzie sat bolt upright. She clutched the comb as if it were her mother's own hand.

'Mum?'

'*I couldn't be prouder of you, luv. You found a new family. And you did it all by yourself.*'

Lizzie couldn't speak. She could see her mother in her mind, but only dimly, as if through clouded glass. But she could tell she was smiling.

'*I always knew you would come to stand on your own two feet. My brave, clever girl. I'm with you, every moment of every day.*'

Right then, Lizzie realized she'd never truly doubted it. The warmth of her mother's love surrounded her like a halo. It had always been there, even during the very worst times.

'Excuse me? Hello?'

A grey-haired customer was peering into the tent, holding the flap back with a worried look on his face.

Lizzie's mother's presence vanished as quickly as a snuffed-out candle flame. Lizzie was suddenly aware of the tears streaming down her face. She'd been crying with joy and she hadn't even realized. Thank goodness for the veil that hid her tears from view.

'Come in,' she said, her voice still shaking with emotion.

This won't do, she told herself. *Pull yourself together, Lizzie. Remember who they've come to see. The Magnificent Lizzie Brown isn't a quivering heap of jelly, is she?*

She coughed and spoke more clearly. 'Do take a seat. How can I assist you?'

'I thought I'd disturbed your trance,' the customer said, looking awkward.

Lizzie waved his concerns away. 'Sometimes I commune with the spirits before I gaze into the future.'

Madame Aurora used to say that, she thought. *Funny thing is, this time I really* was *communing with a spirit – my mum's!*

She took the customer's hand, found his line of life and traced a finger down it. Instantly a vivid scene appeared in her mind of a little cottage under a stormy sky. Rain was lashing down and wind tore through the trees.

'I can see a thatched cottage, somewhere out in the country. Windows with diamond-shaped lead in the panes. And a ruddy great … *ahem* … an impressively large oak tree in the front garden.'

'That's Summerfield!' the man said, amazed. 'It's where Jocelyn and I live.'

Lizzie gasped as a violent gust of wind swayed the oak tree. Instead of swaying back the other way, it kept falling.

There was a dreadful tearing sound as the roots came up. The tree smashed down on the cottage, staving the thatched roof in, crumbling the front wall. From inside the house came the sound of despairing screams.

'What is it? What can you see? Tell me, for heaven's sake!'

Lizzie tightened her grip on his hand. 'That oak tree. Is it still there?'

'Why, yes. It's been there for hundreds of years.'

'Then there's still time. You have to chop it down!'

The man blinked. 'But why? It's not doing any harm.'

'It ain't right now, mister, but it will! I'm telling you, if you don't chop that tree down, there's going to be a storm and it's going to fall right on your house! I saw it happen. And someone was hurt. Hurt bad.'

'Are you saying that's my future?'

'It will be unless you do something,' Lizzie warned.

The man left in such a hurry that he almost forgot to pay. He promised, several times, to chop the tree down.

Alone again, Lizzie let herself relax. Her gift had helped her save someone – probably Jocelyn, the woman the customer had mentioned. She'd heard screaming as the tree came down. Now those screams would never need to be uttered. That gave her a good feeling.

Once her shift was over, it was time for yet another change of clothing, this time into Erin's costume. Ma Sullivan prepared her like she had before, but she had a suspicious look in her eye. Lizzie wondered if she knew what she'd been up to in the cemetery the night before, and was planning to do again tonight.

On her way to the main tent, Lizzie saw Fitzy talking to two men. One was lean, with a top hat and strands of greasy black hair poking out from under it. The other was stockier, with mutton-chop whiskers, a badly healed broken nose and a bowler hat. The lean man had a notebook out and was sucking the end of a fountain pen.

'You have to understand, Mr Fitzgerald, it's not personal,' said the pen-sucker.

'Not personal,' echoed the whiskery one. 'Just business.'

'I just need another week!' Fitzy pleaded. 'You understand unforeseen circumstances, don't you, Leonard?'

'"Mister Crake", if you please. Let's keep it formal, under the circumstances.'

'Formal,' agreed Whiskers.

Lizzie thought he sounded like a parrot.

'But we've always been able to work things out before. We've been doing business together for so long.' Fitzy took off his hat and ran a hand through his hair. 'Can't we at least wait until after tonight's show?'

Malachy tapped Lizzie on the shoulder. 'Those two are loan sharks,' he whispered. 'They lent Pop the cash for the horses and the posters. Now they want it back, with interest.'

'I don't like the look of 'em,' Lizzie whispered back.

'The tall one's Crake, known as Calculating Crake because he works out his profits to the last brass farthing. The other one's Persuading Harry. He used to be a boxer.'

'He "persuades" people to pay up, does he?'

Malachy nodded, looking grim. 'He hasn't got his brass knuckles on yet. That's something, I suppose.'

'Is your father going to be able to pay them?'

'With ticket sales as bad as they are?' Malachy shook his head. 'If it goes on like this, he'll be lucky to clear *half* of what he owes. We just have to hope for a miracle tonight.'

But there was no miracle. What followed was one of the worst nights anyone in the circus could remember. Lizzie watched from behind the beaded curtain. All of the punters had come in but the house was half empty.

'Word must have got out after last night,' said Malachy.

'People must have said not to bother going,' Nora agreed.

Lizzie winced, still feeling like it was her fault. Maybe if she'd put on a better show, the audience would have gone away happier.

Fitzy managed to stir up some half-hearted

applause for the Boissets' opening act. Usually the family's polished skill got the audience gasping in wonder, but this time it fell flat. People folded their arms, talked among themselves, smoked pipes and even read newspapers.

It's like they've made up their minds to have a bad time, no matter what we do, Lizzie thought.

Dru took it personally. As he strode out onto the high wire, he looked determined to impress the audience. Halfway through the penny-farthing routine, he performed a backflip with far too much flashy showmanship, botched the landing completely and nearly fell off the high wire. He landed straddling the wire, his face contorted with pain.

'I can't bear to watch,' Lizzie whispered.

The next acts were no better. Without JoJo, the clowns couldn't perform their normal routine. Their usually hilarious pratfalls met with stony silence. Then, the wild animals were skittish and snarling. Akula the elephant trumpeted and stamped her feet instead of balancing on a ball like a gigantic ballerina. And even Fitzy couldn't get Leo the lion to jump through hoops.

As Lizzie braced herself to go on and face the crowd, Nora came running up to her.

'You may as well go and get changed.'

'What?'

'We can't perform tonight. Victoria's just too wild! She won't calm down no matter what Hari does.'

Lizzie felt relieved, though she tried to look disappointed. 'Poor Fitzy. He's going to burst a blood vessel.'

Although it wasn't her fault, Lizzie felt terrible when she saw Fitzy later on, after the show. He was handing out refunds to punters who had hoped to see the famous Sullivan sisters. After word got out that the ringmaster was giving people their money back, the line of 'disappointed customers' suddenly got a lot longer.

'That's all he needs,' Lizzie muttered. 'He probably hasn't made a penny tonight.'

The Penny Gaff Gang and a handful of circus folk gathered in the tea tent afterwards, still shocked by how badly the evening had gone. They slurped their tea in silence, nobody wanting to be the first to speak.

Eventually, Didi leaned back in his chair with a sigh. 'There's one advantage to a half-empty house. Fewer people to see the circus fall flat on its face.'

'Was it really that bad?' Ma Sullivan asked. Of all the circus folk, she alone seemed satisfied, as if the terrible evening had confirmed her dire warnings.

'It was terrible! The baker's shop routine just doesn't work without old JoJo. We clowns barely got a giggle out of the crowd.'

'At least they liked you!' Collette snapped. 'And clowns are supposed to make fools of themselves – unlike some people!'

Dru glared at her and muttered something in French that Lizzie didn't understand. By the look on Collette's face, it was something rude.

'There's no sense in blaming one another,' Ma Sullivan said. 'It's this site that's to blame.'

Malachy rested his head on his arms. 'I reckon our problems started sooner than that. Back when my dad splashed out all that money on those two horses. It was a gamble and it's not paid off.'

'You can't go blaming the poor horses neither, Mally! Poor dumb beasts. No, it's the Devil's Hound that's spooked them and we all know it. Not to mention the restless souls from that wretched cemetery.' Ma Sullivan came and gave Malachy a pat on the shoulder, to show there were no hard feelings. 'The sooner we move on from this site, the better.'

'Pop won't like it.'

'Ma's only saying what we're all thinking,' grumbled Erin.

'Now, Mally, you'll be a good boy and talk your father round, won't you?' said Ma Sullivan sweetly.

Good thing she doesn't know what the Penny Gaff Gang is planning tonight, thought Lizzie. *If she knew we were heading up to the cemetery, she'd have a fit.*

CHAPTER 12

The gang gathered in Lizzie's caravan for a quick meeting before the cemetery trip.

'Don't go,' begged Nora. 'It's not worth the risk! Especially if we're moving on soon anyway.'

'I suppose that means neither of you are coming?' Lizzie hadn't really expected the twins to come, but it still felt like a let-down.

'Are you joking? Of course we're not,' Nora said.

'Scared of the Devil's Hound?' joked Dru.

'Too right I'm scared of it. But I'm even more scared of me ma.'

'She's got a fearsome temper,' added Erin. 'If she

thought either of us had gone anywhere near that cemetery, she'd boil us alive.'

'You think I'm not scared too?' Lizzie snapped. 'Of course I am. That hound nearly tore my throat out! But we've got to go. Nobody else cares about the poor dead people. Nobody else even knows.'

'That's too bad,' Erin said, 'but we can't help. The dead will have to look out for themselves. Come on, Nora.'

They left the trailer. Nora glanced over her shoulder and whispered, 'Sorry.'

'I can't come either,' Malachy said after an awkward silence.

'Oh, that's just fantastic.'

'Don't look at me like that. I have to help Pop look through the accounts.'

'Because of the debts.' Lizzie understood. 'Sorry, Mal.'

'He thinks we might figure something out,' Malachy said. 'Who knows? Maybe we'll find a solution.'

He got up to leave. As he opened the caravan door, it revealed a startled Becky standing there, about to knock.

She looked nervously from Lizzie to Dru and Hari.

'Are we still going? I thought there'd be more of us.'

'So did I,' Lizzie said. 'Look, if you've changed your mind, it's OK. You don't have to come.'

'I haven't changed my mind,' Becky said, and Lizzie knew right then that the girl was brave enough to face graverobbers and ghosts alike.

'OK!' Dru said, rubbing his hands in excitement. 'We have a team, we have a plan. *Allons-y.*'

'Plan?' Lizzie had missed that part.

Hari held up a length of rope. 'We borrowed this from the spare tent rigging. We climb the wall, sneak up on the graverobbers and catch them in the act.'

'What about the dog?'

'Leave that to me,' Hari said with a calm, knowing smile.

As they approached the cemetery, Lizzie kept a careful watch for any telltale glimpse of light that might be the graverobbers. Nothing showed. The moon was hidden behind clouds tonight and the darkness was almost total.

'We should have brought a light of our own,' she

muttered. 'A lantern, or a candle. Anything.'

'Let your eyes get used to it,' Hari said. 'Learn to see in the dark. Like a cat.'

Dru reached the wall and began to climb. 'Better … we didn't bring … a light.'

'How so?'

'They won't see us coming.' Dru tied the rope around the bough of a nearby tree, then threw it over for the others to use. In moments they were cautiously picking their way through the cemetery, alert to any sight or sound that might mean trouble.

'Stay together,' Lizzie whispered, thinking of Becky. 'We need to check Becky's father's grave first.'

'Follow me. I could take us there with my eyes closed.'

When they arrived at the graveside, Lizzie instantly saw what she'd been dreading. The flowers she had left were nowhere to be seen.

'They've been here,' she said, suddenly feeling very cold.

'They robbed his grave?' Becky's voice trembled. The fiery confidence flooded out of her in a rush of tears as she sank to her knees. 'How … how *could* they?'

'If they're here, we'll catch them,' Lizzie promised.

Becky clutched handfuls of freshly dug earth and squeezed them. She rocked back and forth, moaning. Anyone could see she was in no fit state to take on the graverobbers.

'Why don't you wait here, luv,' Lizzie said, giving her a quick hug. 'We'll go and hunt for the men what done this.'

Becky just nodded weakly, and let loose a fresh flood of tears. *I should never have let her come*, was Lizzie's uncomfortable thought. *She's brave, but she ain't in strong enough shape for this.* It was hardly surprising as the farm girl had only just recovered from smallpox.

Moving faster now without Becky, the three of them – Hari, Dru and Lizzie – crept through the cemetery towards the spot where they'd seen the two men before. Dru grabbed Lizzie's arm and silently pointed out a dark shape passing between the trees.

'Is that them?' whispered Hari.

As if in answer, a low and angry growl came from a nearby clutch of bushes. Lizzie barely had time to register that the hound was closer than she'd expected before it loped out, terrifyingly huge against the night sky.

'The Devil's Hound!' she gasped.

It was right next to them. Last time she'd had a head start, but the enormous dog had still caught up with her. This time, there was no way she could outrun it.

The moon came out from behind a cloud. Now she could see it clearly, a beast like a Great Dane, almost as tall as she was and black as the night sky. She stood paralysed with fear, knowing that those snarling teeth were going to rip through her throat.

The phantom dog snarled, then ran and leaped at her…

Hari's voice rang out, firm and clear. 'Down!'

The dog stopped in its tracks. It looked at Hari and cocked its head, confused.

'Down,' Hari repeated.

Lizzie couldn't believe it. The dog was bigger than the slender boy, but Hari was speaking to him as if he was in charge. Hari's face was calm, showing no fear at all. Slowly, hesitantly, the huge dog sank to the ground.

'Good boy,' Hari said instantly. 'Well done.' He threw the dog a piece of fresh meat from his pocket. Eagerly, the dog gobbled and chomped it up.

'You liked that, didn't you?' Hari crooned. 'Poor thing. Nobody's fed you for a long time, have they?'

He bent down and ruffled the dog's fur as if he had

every right to. To Lizzie's amazement, the dog let him.

'He's doing what he does with the lions!' she whispered to Dru. 'He acts like he's the boss, so they treat him like the boss.'

Within minutes, the 'Devil's Hound' was rolling on his back and licking Hari's face. 'He's showing throat,' Hari explained. 'That means he's submitting to me. In his eyes, I'm pack leader. We can be friends now.'

'I dunno,' Lizzie said nervously. 'You didn't see how he went for Malachy.'

'That wasn't his fault. He's been starved.'

'So he was trying to eat Mal?'

Hari laughed. 'No! He thought he was driving off a rival. He's used to getting by on scraps, so any stranger is a threat who might take his food away.'

Dru dropped to a squat and patted the hound experimentally. 'He seems tame enough now. Like a different dog.'

'Most animals don't want to hurt people. They just need to be treated right.' Hari stood up and held out the back of his hand. The dog sniffed it, then licked it.

'He ain't a ghost dog, that's for sure!' Lizzie said, finally managing to smile. 'Nor one of Ma Sullivan's "coo shees", neither.'

'We just need to find his owners now,' said Hari. 'And with all respect to Ma Sullivan, I doubt either of them is the Devil.'

'How do we find the owners?'

'We follow the dog. Go on, boy! Home!'

The hound looked quizzically at Hari, then padded off through the cemetery.

As they hurried after the hound, moving as silently as they could, Lizzie wondered if the dog wasn't leading them into a trap even now. They were heading deeper into the cemetery than they'd ever gone before. She didn't recognize any of the huge urns, tombs and memorials that they passed.

'Stay out of sight,' whispered Dru. 'The graverobbers could be around any corner.'

All three of them used the tombs for cover, darting quickly from one tomb to the next, only moving on when they knew the coast was clear. The hound, unconcerned, trotted ahead of them as if he were out for an evening walk. In the near-total darkness, it was hard to keep track of where he was going. Lizzie just hoped Hari could keep him under his spell for long enough.

She noticed Dru was passing a length of rope from

one hand to the other. Did he really expect to leap out of the shadows and take the graverobbers by surprise, then tie them up? They weren't dealing with pantomime villains here. These were men desperate enough to dig up the dead and steal from them.

'I think he's getting close,' whispered Hari. 'Good dog.'

Lizzie strode out into the dark. Next moment, her foot caught on something. She fell forwards and stifled a yelp as she landed heavily on her hands and knees on the cold, wet earth.

A fierce pain was shooting up from her ankle. She felt around with her hands and found the temporary grave marker she'd tripped over. As she pulled herself up to sitting, something slimy grazed her hand. Was it the dead body below, coming back to life? Lizzie recoiled in horror, but when she looked down it was only a worm, burying itself deeper into the soil. She shook her head. This cemetery was playing tricks on her mind.

She wobbled to her feet and wiggled her ankle around. It was still sore, but she could walk on it. 'Mal? Dru?' she hissed into the darkness. She looked around, trying to get her bearings. 'Dru, I swear if you're playing games again, I'll skin you alive!'

No answer came. They obviously hadn't heard her stumble, and had moved on. There was nothing for it but to find her own way. Her friends couldn't be much further ahead. Lizzie set off in the direction the dog had been headed in.

The cemetery was like a labyrinth. All around, stone faces with blank eyes stared at her. Statues that the sculptor must have thought would be comforting now looked sinister and strange. They reached out cold marble hands.

A scream rose in her throat, but at the last minute she choked it back. No. She couldn't scream. She mustn't. If the graverobbers were here, it would draw them to where she was. And wouldn't that be a pretty pickle, those two rough men finding her all alone in a cemetery? They'd had no luck drowning her. Lizzie knew they'd be happy to bludgeon her with shovels instead.

Pull yourself together, girl! A graveyard's just a plot of land full of stone statues and monuments, she scolded herself. *All you have to do is find your way through it.*

She breathed deep, slow and steady. Feeling calmer, Lizzie strained to hear the others. She thought she could hear someone whispering just past a tomb with a lion statue on top of it. She started in that direction, but the next moment a vision took hold of her. It was more powerful than anything she'd ever felt while she was reading palms.

Becky was looking up from the bottom of an open grave. She was out of her mind with fear. She let out a terrified scream.

The same scream, coming from across the graveyard, ripped through Lizzie's vision. What she was seeing in her vision was happening right now!

A figure loomed over Becky, a grim shadow in the night.

One of the graverobbers? No – the figure was winged. An angel statue, holding out its arms as if to embrace someone. Lizzie fixed it in her memory.

A lid slammed shut over Becky. Now there was only total darkness, and the knowledge that the girl was trapped in an enclosed space. She banged on the lid but she couldn't get out. She couldn't breathe.

As the vision faded, Lizzie desperately sucked in lungfuls of the night air. The vision was so vivid it had felt like she was suffocating too. Somewhere out there, Lizzie knew, it was happening to Becky for real.

'Hold on, Becky!' she said. 'I'm coming!'

CHAPTER 13

Lizzie set off at a run through the cemetery, heading in the direction Becky's scream had come from.

Before she'd got far, something black burst out of the shrubbery, with Hari close behind. Lizzie yelped and nearly jumped backwards into the bushes. It was the hound, but to her amazement, he was whining, not growling. When he saw her, he barked happily.

'Good boy!' Hari said. 'You found her!'

'Eh?'

'The dog got upset when he realized you weren't with us,' said Dru. 'He ran round in circles then shot off back the way we'd come. And then we heard you scream.'

Hari ruffled the dog's fur. 'He must have followed your scent. Good job he did.'

The hound sniffed Lizzie's hand, then gave it a shy lick. Her fingers trembled.

'Good boy,' she managed to say. 'Are we going to be friends now, then?'

The dog's tail wagged in a great sweeping arc.

'Can you walk?' Dru held out his arm.

'I'm fine!' Lizzie brushed grave dirt and moss from her clothes. The memory of the vision was still burning strong in her mind. 'It's Becky we need to go after now. It wasn't me screaming – it was her. She's in danger!'

'What sort of danger?'

'Someone's got her. I think she's in a grave, running out of air. We need to look for an angel statue.' She mimicked its stance. 'With its arms out, like this.'

'I've seen many angels in this graveyard,' Hari mused, 'but none like that. Dru?'

Dru shook his head. 'Me neither. It could be anywhere.'

Lizzie clenched her fists in frustration. 'We need to search the whole place until we find that angel.'

'Are you crazy?' Hari hissed. 'Even with the hound's

help, that would take hours! Have you seen how *big* this place is?'

Lizzie hated to admit it, but he had a point. There was no way they could search the whole of Kensal Green cemetery in time. They had to move fast. Somewhere, Becky's life was ebbing away. She knew it, as sure as she knew the beating of her own heart.

She glanced up at the tomb beside her. Without a second thought, she grabbed hold of the ornamental carvings on the corner and began to climb. Even with the pain in her ankle, she quickly scrambled to the top. 'Better view from up here.'

'See anything?' Dru sounded impressed.

'Lots of gravestones … some big pots … a sort of temple thing. No angel. There's too many bloomin' hedges and bushes in the way.'

Dru peered in the direction of the 'temple thing', which was a large building with pillars in the front and a peaked roof. 'The cemetery chapel,' he said quietly. 'Lizzie, you're a genius.'

'Come again?'

Dru was already running. 'I can climb up onto the roof. From the top of that, I'll be able to see for miles. *Allons-y!*'

The hound kept pace beside them, but now Lizzie felt safe in his presence. She wondered if Hari was the first person who'd ever been kind to him. Now she thought about it, she'd been a bit of a stray herself when the circus took her in. No wonder the dog was feeling loyal to Hari now.

'We've got more in common than I thought, doggie,' she whispered as she ran.

The chapel didn't look like a church. Its pillared entrance loomed up in front of them like something out of mythology. 'Classical style,' Hari commented. 'It's meant to look like an ancient Greek building.'

Lizzie thought it looked like a tomb for something gigantic. She could easily imagine monstrous remains lying inside: skulls the size of carriages, leg bones huge as tree trunks. *Ma Sullivan was right about one thing*, she thought. *Give me a quaint little country churchyard any day over this place.*

The two wings of the building reached out like arms to either side. They were lower than the rest, with dark openings in the front. Dru passed the rope around one of the columns, wound it around his wrists leaving some slack, and leaned back. By bracing his feet against the column while gripping with the rope, he was able to hitch his way up as easily as if he'd been walking up a hill.

'Can you see Becky?' Lizzie was snappy and impatient now. She knew Dru was doing his best, but they were running out of time. The girl's life was at stake.

Dru silently turned his head like a roosting owl. Then he froze. 'There's a light. Way across the other side of the cemetery. It looks like a lantern.'

Lizzie held her breath waiting for Dru to speak again.

At last, he did. 'I see three people. No – two. The other one's not moving. Two and a statue.'

'An angel statue?'

'Yes, I think so. Yes! Holding out its arms, *comme ça*. Like it's saying, "Come here, *mon amour*."'

'That's the one! That's where Becky is! Get down here, fast!'

Dru jumped back down to the lower roof. Using his rope as a brake, he skidded down the column in seconds flat. 'Fast enough for you?' he panted.

Together they raced through the graveyard in the direction of the light Dru had seen. *Don't worry, Becky*, Lizzie thought. *We're coming. Please don't be afraid, wherever you are.*

When they'd almost reached the light, Dru whispered, 'Hari and I will go in opposite directions, and then we'll all close in on them.'

When the boys went off their separate ways, Lizzie noticed a sprawled figure lying motionless behind a tombstone, a single arm flung out as if to point out some unseen danger. She couldn't see clearly in the darkness, but the figure was wearing white, just as Becky had been.

'Becky!' she shouted and dashed towards her. The figure, face down, didn't move, and Lizzie had the horrible thought that she was too late. Was she unconscious? As she reached down to roll Becky over, she noticed that her friend's hair didn't look quite right. It looked more black than brown in the moonlight.

Lizzie grabbed a cold shoulder and pulled the body over. The face of a dead woman rolled up into view, pale and glistening. There were patches of green on her cheeks. She must have lain dead in the ground for a while. As Lizzie stared in horror, the corpse's mouth fell open and a beetle clambered out of it.

Lizzie shoved her knuckles into her mouth to keep from screaming. She turned away, squeezing her eyes shut, fighting the sudden urge to be sick.

Ahead of her, the hound began to bark furiously.

'The ruddy dog's back at last,' a gruff voice said, from somewhere close to the light. 'What's it makin' all that noise for?'

'God knows,' said another voice. 'I told you we should have drowned it in the canal. It's useless, that dog.'

'Give it a smack.'

'I done that loads of times. Last time it bit me. Save your breath for work!'

They were the two men from the canal. Lizzie was sure of it. Leaving her grisly find where it lay, she crouched down and began to move stealthily towards the men, keeping out of sight behind the gravestones. She could just make them out now, dark shadows in front of the light. They were shovelling.

'I think it's seen something,' the first voice said. 'We should check.'

'Who's going to come out 'ere on a night like this?' the other scoffed.

'Maybe it's hungry.'

'It can have a bite of the cold meat we dug up, then.' They both laughed in a filthy way that made Lizzie bite her lip in anger.

Dru and Hari were advancing on the graverobbers too, behind tombstones of their own. The hound stopped barking and lay down, whining softly, as if he was afraid. *He's worried about Hari*, Lizzie suddenly thought. *He knows these men are dangerous.*

Soon there was nothing but a single headstone between her and the villains. She crouched, heart pounding, listening to the sounds of soil sliding from their shovels into the open grave. Dirt rattled against something wooden.

Realization suddenly hit her. *Becky's in the coffin. They're burying her alive!*

'Stop!' Lizzie screamed. She ran for the man nearest to her – the older one – seized hold of his shovel and nearly tugged it out of his hands. They staggered back and forth at the edge of the grave. Lizzie glanced down into it and saw the coffin was almost completely covered with earth.

'It's that bloomin' girl again!' the man yelled. 'Get off!'

'You're too nosy for your own good,' grunted the other. 'There's room enough in that there grave for two of you. You can go and keep your friend company.'

Holding his shovel like a club, the younger man ran

round the grave and came at Lizzie from behind. Now she was caught between the pair of them. All she could do was let go of the shovel and try to duck and dodge as best she could.

'Hold still!' The younger graverobber slammed his shovel down like a sledgehammer, trying to smash Lizzie's skull in. She scrambled away, falling back into the mound of freshly dug earth. Soil trickled into her boots as she struggled to stand up.

The graverobber gave her an ugly grin. 'Chop, chop, little worm,' he said, twisting the shovel in his hands so as to use its edge.

He swung it again, using it like an axe now. Lizzie rolled and the shovel sank into the earth where she'd been seconds before, showering her with dirt.

'Finish her off, Jimmy!' shouted the other, leaning on his shovel like a cane.

The man laughed and stood over Lizzie, with one leg on either side so she couldn't roll away. He raised the shovel like a guillotine blade. 'Don't worry. Her head's comin' off.'

Helpless, Lizzie looked up at the glinting metal, wondering if it was the last thing she'd ever see. Then, from the shadows, Dru flung himself onto the man's back. The man gave a shrill scream of surprise as if the Devil himself had leaped up from the grave to carry him off. Dru bit his ear, making him howl even more, and Lizzie quickly scrambled away.

The man dropped his shovel and grabbed Dru's hair, trying to throw him off. As the other graverobber approached to confront her, Lizzie grabbed the fallen shovel and jumped down into the grave, out of his reach.

'Hit 'im, Jeff!' screamed the struggling man, lurching to the left and right as he tried to buck Dru off his back. 'Get 'im off me!'

The other swung his shovel clumsily at Dru's dangling leg. Dru nimbly hoisted himself onto the man's shoulders. The flat of the shovel whacked the man's knee. He shrieked in pain.

Dru vaulted off the man's shoulders, landing perfectly on the soft earth. Even without an audience to cheer him on, the acrobat's timing was impeccable.

'Sorry, Jimmy. I couldn't 'elp it!' the graverobber whined.

Lizzie knew she wouldn't be able to get the coffin lid open. Even if she hadn't been standing on it, there was just too much earth weighing it down. So she frantically began to shovel the dirt back out, flinging it over her shoulder. She heard yells and howls of pain from up above and hoped that Dru would be all right.

Then she heard him cry out as he was thrown to the ground. '*Salauds!*' he gasped. 'Let go!'

'Got you now, you little bleeder,' one of the men grunted. 'Twist his arm around a bit more, Jeff. See if you can't break it.'

'Hari!' Dru roared. 'What are you waiting for?'

There was a deep growl from somewhere close by.

'Get them!' Hari shouted.

With a flurry of barks and snapping jaws, the hound turned on his former masters. Lizzie heard ripping cloth as he got one of them by the leg. The man screamed and struggled. 'Call it off! Call your bloomin' dog off!'

'That dog's ours!' gasped the other, backing away. 'You got no right!'

'He doesn't seem to think he's your dog any more,' Hari said coldly. 'I wonder why?'

'I'm bleeding!' wailed the fallen graverobber. The dog was mauling his leg like a tug-of-war with a tree branch. 'Jimmy, for Gawd's sake, come and help!'

'No chance, mate,' said Jimmy. 'I'm off.'

'You ruddy coward!'

Jimmy started to run. All Hari had to do was whistle, and the dog knew what to do. He released the moaning graverobber, who rolled over clutching his leg, and bounded off after Jimmy.

A single snap, a scream, and a sound of a man falling over told Lizzie that the hound had caught his prey. That took care of the graverobbers. Now there was only Becky to find. If she was even down there…

Lizzie threw spadeful after spadeful of earth out of the grave. Without warning, her shovel struck wood. *The coffin.*

'Still got that rope, Dru?' Hari called from above her.

'Of course.'

'Good. Let's tie these two up.'

Lizzie stood astride the coffin and tried to pull the lid open. It didn't give. Her fingers felt the bumpy heads of iron nails. They must have nailed it shut.

Determined not to give up, she worked the shovel's edge back and forth into the crack below the lid, then pulled it back like a crowbar. With a low groan, the lid grudgingly came up half an inch.

Encouraged, Lizzie gripped the lid tightly and pulled with all her strength. A slow landslide of earth slid off the rising lid. Suddenly it began to rise even more as someone pushed it up from within. Wood splintered and cracked, and then finally – as Lizzie gave the lid a frantic tug – it came off completely.

CHAPTER 14

Becky lay gasping in the coffin below her. She sat up like a jack-in-the-box. Looking up at Lizzie with tear-streaked eyes, she asked, 'Am I a ghost now?

'I'm dead, aren't I?' Becky sobbed, sounding close to madness. 'You can talk to ghosts and I must be one.'

'You're fine.' Lizzie patted her back. 'Just breathe. Take your time.'

Becky flung her arms around Lizzie, hugging so tight it hurt. 'They put me in the coffin!'

'I know. Hush. It's all right.'

Becky's fingers tightened like claws. She breathed heavily. 'It was so dark … I couldn't even move in that box … I screamed and screamed but nobody came.'

Lizzie struggled out of Becky's grasp with difficulty. 'Let's get you out of this hole, quick as you like. Up you get.'

Lizzie helped Becky out of the grave. Becky kept babbling as they made their way up. 'I could hear the earth landing on the coffin lid, *boom*, like a drum. And I could hear them laughing.' A sudden new fear came over Becky's face. 'Those men! They'll come back, they'll get you too!'

'Oh no, they won't,' Lizzie told her confidently. 'Come and see.'

She showed Becky where the two graverobbers lay. Dru and Hari had done a thorough job with the rope. The graverobbers were swaddled up as tight as flies in a spider's web.

'Havin' a gloat, are yer?' one of them leered.

Becky turned away. 'I can't look at them,' she said hoarsely. 'Not after what they did. They're beasts.'

Lizzie walked down the hill with her a few paces until the graverobbers were out of sight. Then Becky sank to the ground and began weeping hysterically.

'Can you tell me what happened?' Lizzie asked, as gently as she could.

Becky nodded and wiped her nose. 'After you all left me by my dad's grave, I felt a bit silly. I mean, crying wasn't going to help, was it? So I thought I'd try to catch up with you, but it was too dark to see and I couldn't find you anywhere.'

'That was brave,' Lizzie said, trying to lift Becky's spirits a bit.

'Then I saw a light,' she went on. 'I thought it might be you, so I went closer, and I saw those two men. They'd dug up some poor woman's grave and I saw them throw her body on the ground, with no more respect than if she were a sack of potatoes! It made me so angry, and then I thought of my dad, and that made it worse. I just ran at them, yelling my head off.'

'Blimey!' Lizzie was genuinely impressed now. 'Bet you gave them a scare!'

Becky laughed a little through her tears. 'I did too. I gave them such an earful! Told them I'd report them, that they'd never get away with it. Then the big one, the really nasty one, he said, "There's two of us and only one of you, love, and you won't be reporting nothing." Then they … they…' She couldn't say it. Becky began to tremble violently.

Lizzie finished the sentence for her. 'They put

you in the empty coffin?'

Becky nodded. She said something so faintly that Lizzie had to ask her to say it again.

'They said nobody would miss me.' Becky looked up at the moon, grimacing in tearful misery. 'And it's true! I don't matter to anyone any more, now my pa's dead! Who'd even notice if I just vanished off the face of the earth?'

Lizzie hugged her. 'Of course people would miss you. What a thing to say!'

As Becky clung to Lizzie as if she feared the ground would rear up and swallow her again, the hound came trotting over curiously. It seemed to sense that the girl was distressed and nuzzled its nose up under her hand, with a soft questioning whine.

'Hello,' Becky said, surprised. 'Where did you spring from, eh?' She stroked the dog's sleek fur, hesitated and stopped, unsure if she should go on. But the dog pawed at her, clearly wanting more attention.

'He likes you,' Lizzie said, pleased.

Becky carried on fussing the dog, scratching his chest until he beat his leg happily on the ground. The dog was calming Becky down, so Lizzie silently got up and went to see what was happening with Dru and Hari.

They were in the middle of a whispered debate. 'We should go and wake the sexton up,' Hari insisted. 'It's his job to look after the graveyard. He'll know what to do.'

'And leave these two?' Dru jerked a thumb at the tied-up graverobbers.

'We can't bring them with us, can we?'

'Maybe we should chuck 'em in the grave,' Lizzie said coldly, and the way the villains' eyes widened in fear gave her a sweet feeling of revenge. 'Oh, don't worry, you two,' she told them. 'We're better than that.'

After checking that the ropes were securely tied, they all went to find the sexton's cottage, leaving the prisoners behind to curse each other's foolishness and their own bad luck. Dru remembered seeing a little house close to the outer wall, and sure enough, that proved to be the right place. The cottage looked cosy and comfortable considering it was on the edge of a graveyard.

It took three rounds of knocking before a window opened and the sexton stuck his head out. Lizzie tried not to laugh at his floppy nightcap.

'What's this all about? Have you any idea what

time it is?'

'Sorry to bother you, sir,' Lizzie said, 'but there's graverobbers in your cemetery.'

'Graverobbers?'

'I knew it, Harold!' squawked a woman's voice from inside. 'Didn't I tell you there was something going on? Funny lights and a dog barking. I said it an 'undred times. But would you go and look? Would you heck!'

'I'll be right out,' the sexton said sourly.

He opened the door to them in a hastily pulled-on overcoat, still with the nightcap on his head. He looked from one to the other of them, deeply suspicious. 'Well?'

'We caught 'em in the act, sir,' Lizzie said. 'They'd dug up a lady! But we fought 'em, and we won, and now they're all tied up. You can see for yourself.'

The sexton looked like he believed her, but then he frowned deeply. 'And what on earth were you all doing in the cemetery in the first place, may I ask?'

They couldn't possibly tell him the truth. Lizzie thought quickly. 'We were going after our dog!' she lied.

Becky realized what Lizzie was doing and nodded. She gave the huge dog a pat and said, 'He's a naughty boy.'

'In the middle of the night?' growled the sexton. 'Seems an odd time to walk a dog.'

'He ran away!' Lizzie said. 'Right out of the yard, down the street, and off into the cemetery. So we went to look for him, and we caught two blokes in the middle of robbing a grave. You've got to come with us!'

The sexton sighed. 'Very well. But if this is some sort of prank, there'll be hell to pay.'

'Harold?' came the voice from within, making the man wince. 'Are you still standing about? Get after them!'

'I'm going now, dear,' he sing-songed. Grumpily, he followed the four of them back the way they'd come.

His attitude changed the moment he saw the tied-up men. Instead of being merely irritable, he was coldly furious. 'You dare to desecrate this holy place?'

They yelled and begged for him to help, claiming, 'We never done nothing!' and, 'It were them kids, mister!'

Lizzie showed him to where the lady's corpse lay nearby, discarded like a piece of rubbish.

'That's Cecily Musgrove,' the sexton said. He took off his cap and clutched it to his chest in shock.

'She was buried only a week ago.'

'It weren't us,' insisted the younger graverobber.

'And I suppose these children dug a body up all by themselves, did they? If I were you I'd hold my tongue. You're in enough trouble as it is.' The sexton turned to the children. 'I need your help.'

'*Bien sûr,*' Dru said gallantly.

'Run back to my cottage and tell my wife to fetch the police. I'm going to wait here with these two. If they try to escape, so help me I'll do them an injury.'

'Right you are!' With a wink and a grin, Lizzie and her friends dashed back towards the cottage.

The next few hours passed in a blur. It was well past midnight now, and Lizzie was growing drowsy. She refused the sexton's wife's offer to catch a few hours of sleep on the wooden settle, though it looked inviting. She wanted to be there when the police came.

Eventually, they arrived – two officers in stiff black uniforms, eager for something to liven up their night-time beat. One of them bundled the graverobbers off, menacing them with his truncheon, while the other asked the children questions and took notes. Yes, the graverobbers had tried to bury a young girl alive. Yes, they had been digging up the graveyard for weeks now. And yes, Lizzie was indeed the same Lizzie Brown who'd been the talk of London when she unmasked the notorious Phantom.

The policeman took Lizzie aside. 'Just between the two of us,' he whispered, 'how'd you do it?'

'Do what?'

'How'd you know where to find these two, and catch 'em in the act?'

'I told you,' Lizzie said innocently. 'Our dog ran away and we went to fetch him.'

'Ah yes…' The copper smirked knowingly. 'Your dog. Well, wasn't that lucky.' A thoughtful expression came over his face. 'It's quite a collar, this. I've been waiting for something big to come up for a while. Maybe we can help each other.'

'I don't follow.'

He wrote down a name and address on a piece of paper, tore it off and gave it to her. 'If you happen to have any other insights, just come see me at the station. Not a word to anyone else, understand?' He winked and tapped his nose.

Lizzie looked at him blankly.

'You scratch my back, I'll scratch yours,' the police officer said. 'A good tip-off could make my career and I'm willing to pay for it.'

Lizzie felt a little queasy at that. *My powers are for helping people*, she thought, *not for getting coppers promotions.* She tucked the paper away without looking at it.

The sexton helpfully unlocked the cemetery gates to let them out. The black night sky was changing to a washed-out dim blue as they made their way up the path, so tired they felt like falling over in their tracks.

'The sun's coming up,' Hari pointed out. 'We've been out all night.'

Becky yawned and hugged Lizzie goodbye. 'You saved my life,' she whispered. 'I'll never forget that.'

'I'll see you again soon,' Lizzie promised. 'Those men won't go disturbing sacred ground any more. I hope that helps your dad rest easy.'

Lizzie, Dru and Hari made their way back to the circus, with the hound still trotting at Hari's heels. Was this really the same animal she'd run away from, all burning eyes and bared teeth? In the growing light, she could see he was only a dog. A big one, yes, but with needy brown eyes. Not to mention the lolling tongue that made him look daft.

'You shouldn't have fed him, Hari,' Dru said, shaking his head.

'Why not? He was half starved, poor thing.'

'But he'll never leave you alone now.'

'I don't mind,' said Hari. 'He can come back to the circus with me.'

'Won't your dad have something to say about that?' Lizzie asked.

'My father won't mind. What's one more animal in our menagerie?'

Lizzie laughed. 'He ain't exactly a performer, though, is he? What's he good for?'

'Security?' Hari laughed, too. 'We could do with a watchdog. People might give us a bit less bother if Dog here was on the job.'

Lizzie thought of the debt collectors, and imagined the hound chasing them off the site. It was a pleasing thought.

'Is that his name, then?' Dru said. 'Dog?'

'Until I think of a better one,' Hari said. 'I'd call him Dru, but that name's taken.'

'No, call him Dru!' Dru said with a grin. 'Then

everyone will say "Lizzie's chasing after Dru again".' Lizzie felt her face grow red at Dru's teasing. Why did he have to do that? He knew she liked him. Boys could be so stupid.

'We should call him Shadow,' she said suddenly. It was the perfect name. The boys looked at one another and nodded.

When they reached the circus, Hari took Shadow for an early breakfast while Dru crawled off to bed in the Boisset trailer. Lizzie felt so tired that her clothes seemed to hang heavily on her body, but she resisted the comfort of her bed. She had someone to see to first.

She went to the Sullivans' caravan and quietly let herself in. The Sullivans were packed into their bunks like sardines. Sean was snoring, but the others somehow slept through it.

A shape sat up from a bundle of blankets. It was Nora. 'Lizzie?' she whispered. 'Is that you? I haven't slept a wink…'

'Of course it's me,' Lizzie whispered back.

'I had nightmares,' Nora murmured sleepily. 'Oh, Lizzie, why'd you have to go back to that place? I'm so glad you're safe … an' the Devil's Hound didn't get you…'

'You'll get to meet the Devil's Hound tomorrow,' Lizzie whispered into her ear. 'It turns out he's a big old softie.'

'Hmmm?' Nora mumbled, confused. She rolled over. In seconds, the sound of snoring drifted up.

Lizzie lay on the floor of the trailer, readying herself to get up again. Exhaustion dragged at her bones. *I should go to my own bed*, she thought.

But the Sullivans' trailer was so cosy and felt so safe that she fell asleep right where she was, lying on the bare wooden planks with only her hair for a pillow.

CHAPTER 15

When Lizzie finally woke, her first thought was: *I'm back in my own bed.* She sat up. Bright sunlight was streaming through the windows. At the end of the bed, Erin and Nora were waiting with a fresh cup of tea.

'Pa found you on our floor,' Erin explained. 'He carried you back here.'

Lizzie rubbed her eyes. 'I must have been dead to the world.'

'You were!'

Lizzie downed the tea in one long series of gulps, wiped her mouth, looked out of the window and felt a jolt of panic. 'What time is it?'

'It's after ten,' Nora said.

'Ten? I must have slept for hours! Why didn't anyone wake me up sooner?'

'Everyone wanted to let the hero get some rest,' Erin grinned.

Memories of last night came swimming back into her mind. 'Oh,' was all she could say. 'I s'pose Dru and Hari are up, then.'

'The whole circus is buzzing!' Nora said. 'Everyone's heard about the graverobbers, and the arrests. Even Fitzy's in a good mood.'

'The Magnificent Lizzie Brown has done it again,' Erin said, laughing.

Lizzie sank back into her welcoming bedclothes with a happy sigh. 'Cheers for the tea. The Magnificent Lizzie Brown's going to have a bit more kip.' She stretched out and rolled over in the sunlight like a lounging cat.

'Oh no she's not,' said Nora.

'But you said I was a hero,' Lizzie complained.

'Even heroes need to rehearse. You're still standing in for Erin, remember? There's a show tonight.'

Lizzie groaned and pulled her pillow down over her face. 'Everyone's going to be starin' at me.'

'That's the idea,' said Erin, standing *en pointe* and raising a leg gracefully. 'They're the audience, you're the star.'

'Co-star,' Nora corrected.

Lizzie wondered what would happen if she just stayed under the bedclothes for the rest of the day. It was so nice here, warm and dark. Nobody could see her; nobody could laugh at her making a fool of herself.

Nora had once explained that she and Erin were Leos, the sign of the lion. It explained why they loved the limelight so much. Leos were often outgoing and showy. But Lizzie was a Scorpio, the sign of the scorpion. Scorpios were meant to be dark and secretive, hiding away from the sight of others. Lizzie wasn't sure if she believed in astrology or not. It seemed too much like the kind of rubbish Madame Aurora used to prattle about. But she knew she was cut from very different cloth to the twins and there was no getting around it.

The trick to getting up when you wanted to stay in bed was to do it quickly. Lizzie flung back the covers and dressed herself, while Erin and Nora went to tell Ma Sullivan that she was up.

Breakfast was waiting for her in the tea tent: porridge, bacon, another mug of tea, black pudding, scrambled eggs and toast. 'Eat hearty,' Pa Sullivan smiled over his newspaper. 'An empty sack won't stand.'

Ma Sullivan folded her arms and gave Lizzie a piercing look. 'So. You've taken to gallivanting around in cemeteries now, have you?'

'And if she hadn't?' Pa Sullivan spoke up. 'There'd be two villains walking around free, instead of being in gaol.'

'Yeah. Give Lizzie some credit, Mrs S!' cried Rice Pudding Pete. 'She's done a good thing, she has.'

'Good never comes from bad, you mark my words.' Ma Sullivan retreated behind the counter, obviously the only person left on the site who frowned on Lizzie's behaviour. 'You may think you're the bee's knees, laughin' at the old tales and their wisdom, but I warn you, the Devil's Hound is real.'

'I know he is,' Lizzie said with a grin. 'I met him. And now he's joined the circus!'

Ma Sullivan's mouth fell open.

The girls headed into the show tent to practise for the evening's performance. Hari was already waiting with

Albert and Victoria. A group of clowns and stagehands were sitting in the stalls, munching on sandwiches. Normally they'd be chatting and joking during their break. But in JoJo's absence, the clowns were unusually quiet, clearly worried about their gravely ill friend.

Lizzie winced. Did they have to eat their lunch here? Performing in front of an audience was bad enough without having to rehearse in front of one too.

Nora noticed Lizzie's discomfort. 'You've got to get used to it, Lizzie,' she sighed. 'Besides, the clowns are the perfect test audience for what we've got in mind.'

'Test audience?' Lizzie put two and two together. 'Wait. Have you been talking to Malachy?'

'Yes,' Nora admitted. 'Come on, it was a good idea he had. And the usual routine wasn't working so well.'

'Great. Now I'm going to be making a fool of myself on purpose.'

'Isn't that better than doing it by accident?' Erin asked with a grin.

Nora clapped her hands. 'Let's start. We're going to make it more of a comedy act, just like Malachy suggested. Lizzie, you try to do the stunts and mess them up, then I'll do them properly.'

'Mess them up how?'

'Wave your arms and legs about like JoJo does,' came a shout from the audience. It was Didi the clown. 'Wobble back and forth. Make faces. Exaggerate everything.'

'Don't worry about falling off until the very end,' Nora said. 'We'll make sure you've got a safety rope. Just land on your bum on Victoria's back, drop the juggling clubs, that sort of thing.'

'And at the very end, when I do fall off?'

'Someone will catch you when you fall.'

'I hear Dru's volunteered for that duty,' Erin said lightly.

'That may well be true,' smiled Nora, with satisfaction.

Lizzie pondered that. She still wasn't convinced. 'Me breaking me neck isn't funny, though. Who's going to laugh at that?'

'Let me show you something, love,' said Didi, coming down from the stalls and making for the band's equipment. 'Rice Pudding Pete, kindly do a pratfall for me.'

Pete slipped on an imaginary banana skin and landed heavily on his backside. Lizzie gave a weak smile.

'Let's try that again,' Didi said. This time, as

Pete slipped and landed, Didi played a resounding *boinnggggg* on the drums. Lizzie laughed out loud. 'I see what you mean.'

'It's the music what makes it funny,' Pete said with a wink. 'Every time you go arse-over-teakettle, there'll be a noise to make 'em laugh in the stalls.'

'So,' Nora said, 'are we ready?'

They managed ten minutes of practice. Lizzie found, to her surprise, that clowning suited her much more than serious performance. The onlookers gave her a round of applause every time she fluffed a routine. Before long, she was grinning despite herself.

And then Victoria bucked. Nora gasped an 'Oh, no!' and quickly dismounted. Hari came running up.

'She's not on the turn again, is she?' Lizzie asked.

'I do not understand it,' Hari said. Victoria stamped and whinnied even under his gentle hands. 'Outside, she is calm. In here, she is skittish.'

Lizzie thought about Shadow the dog, and what Hari had said about him. Animals usually had a good reason for behaving strangely. What could it possibly be? Shadow had been starved and mistreated, but Victoria had been given nothing but star treatment ever since they'd set up the circus here.

Star treatment. The words echoed in Lizzie's mind. She looked from Victoria to the group of circus folk sitting in the audience. *She's the star of the show, just like I am. But nobody asked her if she wanted to be a big star, did they?*

Lizzie remembered the first time Victoria had been spooked. It was at the entrance to the cemetery, while the funeral procession had been passing by. Maybe ghosts weren't to blame at all. Maybe the problem was that everyone in the procession had been staring at them. At her!

'Victoria,' she guessed, 'you don't like being looked at any more than I do, do you? Poor girl, you've got stage fright too!'

Nora came over to her, looking curious. 'You've had an idea?'

'I think I know why Victoria's playing up. She don't like being stared at!'

Victoria shook her head, making a whickering noise that sounded like disgust.

Nora's mouth widened into an O. 'You've got a point, there. Every single time she's acted up, there were people watching! The cemetery gates, the field, the show, and now this!'

'But what about last night?' Lizzie wondered. 'She didn't even go on, she was that panicked. Who was watching her then?'

'The debt collectors,' Hari said with a sigh. 'And half a dozen of us circus people who were there to keep an eye on them. I think Lizzie's right.'

'So what do we do about it? We can't hide the audience away, can we?' Lizzie looked into Victoria's sad dark eyes, and felt sorry for her. 'Poor thing. You couldn't say what the problem was, could you? I wish we'd guessed it sooner.'

'This might not be that tough a problem to crack,' Nora said happily. 'Give me just a moment.' She rushed off, then came back after a few minutes holding something like a harness.

'Blinkers?' Lizzie guessed.

'Maybe if she can't see the crowd, she won't get upset.'

Before they could put the theory to the test, Malachy appeared at the entrance. 'Special meeting in the tea tent! Attendance mandatory for everyone!' He grinned at Lizzie. 'And that counts double for you.'

* * *

'Blimey,' Lizzie whispered as they saw Fitzy, who was standing on a box and beaming at the gathered crowd. 'If he was any happier you could stick him on a cliff top and use him as a bloomin' lighthouse.'

'Ladies and gentlemen!' called Fitzy. 'Boys and girls. Scruffy ha'p'orths. Dear friends, one and all...'

'Get on with it!' someone shouted. A peal of laughter followed, from Fitzy too.

'I draw your attention to this special edition of the *London Evening Post*,' he declared. 'Please be so good as to read the headline.' He held the newspaper up so everyone could see it.

Lizzie mouthed the words along with everyone else:

CIRCUS CHILDREN APPREHEND GRAVEROBBERS

Desecration Ended

By Valiant Youths of Fitzy's Travelling Circus.

Lizzie pushed through to the front for a better look. An artist had provided a sketch, using a lot of imagination. It showed a group of children in circus costumes – a clown, an acrobat, a lion-tamer – surrounding a grave. An ogreish-looking man was climbing out, with a corpse slung over his shoulder.

'I can't take my eyes off you lot for a minute, can I?' Fitzy laughed. 'Now, I don't want to get anyone in trouble with their folks, so I won't ask the heroes to identify themselves. But I think we can all guess who they were.'

A lot of feet were shuffled and a fair few people whistled in mock innocence. Lizzie looked around at all the smiling faces and grinned bashfully. Even Ma Sullivan couldn't keep her stony face on any more, and broke into a smile.

Fitzy read aloud from the paper, which told a slightly garbled version of the story. Lizzie didn't remember any heroic boy clown tripping the graverobbers up and sending them tumbling into a grave, for one thing. But everyone turned to look at her when the story mentioned a mysterious 'fortune-teller' with 'powers quite beyond the common table-tappers and Mr Sludges of London society.'

'What's a Mister Sludge?' Lizzie asked Malachy.

'He's a fake medium from a Robert Browning poem,' Malachy whispered. 'It means the papers think you're genuine. I'd brace yourself for a lot more customers if I were you.'

Fitzy's voice rang out. 'Now, some of you might be thinking, "Cor blimey, I bet all that publicity in the papers has done wonders for ticket sales." And you'd be right! We've sold a great many tickets for tonight's show.' He looked right at Lizzie, and his eyes gleamed with a wonderful light. 'In fact, we have sold *every single one* of tonight's tickets!'

'We're sold out?' Mario exclaimed.

'Packed to the rafters!' Fitzy raised his hat. Everyone broke out cheering and clapping.

Lizzie was thrilled for Fitzy, but she just didn't feel like celebrating. Malachy gave Lizzie a hug. But when she stiffened, he took his arm away.

'What's the matter?'

'I'm not sure,' she muttered. 'I just feel … sort of wrong.'

'Sorry. Everyone's looking at you, aren't they? I know you don't like that.'

'No, it's not the attention. I don't mind that, not from friends. It's something else.' She turned to leave. Malachy started after her, but Lizzie said, 'I probably just need to get some rest.'

Outside the tent, in the cool air, Lizzie listened to the sounds of celebration. The mood had shifted, and about time too. It was grand to see Fitzy full of hope again. So where was this unsettled feeling coming from?

She still had to perform tonight, but no, that wasn't what was gnawing at her. The graverobbers were safely locked away, so they wouldn't be out for revenge. That wasn't it either. Deep down, it felt like something was still wrong. Perhaps her clairvoyant powers could help her see clearly…

Lizzie needed to be on her own. Celebrations and rehearsals would just have to wait. She climbed inside her trailer, closed the door and sat down on the bed. A wave of fatigue swept over her – she badly needed a nap.

She began to clear the clutter off her bed. Hairbrush, book, loose change … and the horse brass Becky had given her. She picked it up, thinking that she'd put it away in a drawer – and a vision took hold of her mind, so powerful it forced her to her knees.

She saw Becky's father, flat on his back on a metal table. All around him lay peculiar implements: steel tongs, a saw, strange metal items like spikes and clips. He was white as flour and not moving.

'*Help me,*' his voice pleaded in Lizzie's mind. '*I cannot rest. Make them put me back!*'

'Where are you?' Lizzie cried out. 'Ain't you buried?'

'*Help me! She's coming…*'

Next moment, the hunched figure of Mrs Crowe, the housekeeper at Doctor Gladwell's, leaned into the vision. Her eyes narrowed and her nostrils twitched, as if she could smell Lizzie watching her.

'… *coming to cut meeeee!*' wailed the ghostly voice.

Slowly, Mrs Crowe wiped a bright metal object clean on a wad of cotton. She raised it up into the light, and Lizzie felt a chill as she saw what it was…

A terrifyingly sharp scalpel!

CHAPTER 16

A knock at the door made Lizzie start. 'Come in?' she croaked, still feeling shaky.

Malachy peered in, a cup of tea in his hand. 'I thought maybe I ought to check on you. When you don't feel right, there's usually something psychic going on.'

'Thanks,' she said, with genuine gratitude. She stood up, felt dizzy and sat down again.

'Having one of your turns?' Malachy passed her the tea and watched curiously, as if he half expected her head to start spinning round.

The tea moistened her throat and made it easier to

speak. 'I had a vision,' she said. 'A horrible one. Seems like they've all been horrible lately.'

She described what she'd seen. The memory of Becky's father's pale, cold flesh made her skin crawl. And his voice … there wasn't a shred of hope left in it.

'Well,' Malachy eventually said. 'What do you make of it?'

'I don't know.' Lizzie rubbed her forehead. It was damp with sweat. 'I thought all this was over. It's not, though, is it?'

'It might be. Maybe what you're seeing now is the past.'

'The past?' Lizzie took another sip.

'Think about it,' Malachy persisted. 'We know Becky's dad is down at the cemetery, don't we? They dug him up, took his stuff, but when they didn't find any jewels or gold, they chucked it away in the canal. So you must be seeing visions of when he was alive.'

That didn't sound right. 'He was so pale!'

'So was JoJo,' Malachy pointed out. 'Becky's dad must have gone to Doctor Gladwell's when he was ill. Mrs Crowe probably helped the doctor care for him.'

'I dunno.' Lizzie hadn't seen the body move at all. And usually her visions of the past had a slightly fuzzy quality, whereas this vision was sharp and crisp.

But so far as Malachy was concerned, the discussion was over. 'Back to work for me,' he said, dusting himself off. 'Lots to do tonight. It's a full house, remember?'

'Malachy—'

'Yes?' He looked very tired.

'Never mind.'

Once Malachy had left, Lizzie lay down and listened to the sounds of preparation coming from all around the field. She knew she badly needed to rehearse some more, but the show tent would be busy now, and there was nowhere else to practise. Besides, the vision was lingering in her mind, nagging her to act.

'What am I meant to do?' she murmured.

Should she hold the horse brass again, and try to talk to Becky's father?

No. She didn't want to hear that despairing moan again. Let Malachy think what he liked. She was convinced the man she'd seen had been dead. Did that mean his body was at Doctor Gladwell's house right now, then? But if it was, what on earth was Mrs Crowe doing with it?

A horrible thought came back into her mind. Erin had had a theory about dead bodies, and the kind of people who had uses for them. 'Witchcraft,' she'd said. 'There's things a witch can do with a dead man's skin, if they get it all off in one piece.'

Lizzie shuddered. Mrs Crowe certainly looked like a witch. And she'd had a sharp scalpel in the vision ...

As Lizzie's horror grew, JoJo's words came back to her. He'd warned her to stay away, just before Mrs Crowe had come and thrown them out. What was it he'd said? Something about being stabbed to death with needles...

Witches make wax figures of people, don't they? Lizzie suddenly remembered Ma Sullivan telling her this. *They're called 'poppets'. And they stab them with needles, so the victim dies a lingering death...*

'JoJo!' she cried, leaping to her feet. Show or no show, she had to go and visit Doctor Gladwell's house, right now. If Mrs Crowe really was a witch, the clown's life was in grave danger.

Doctor Gladwell's house loomed over the surrounding hedge, its dark windows filled with secrets. Lizzie lingered beside the main gate for a few minutes, catching her breath after the journey, working up the courage to go inside. She couldn't get that gleaming scalpel out of her mind.

Once she was certain nobody was coming or going, she hurried through the gate. The front door was ahead of her, inside its ornamental porch, with the bench nearby – empty now, she saw. Gravel paths surrounded the house, and there were big rhododendron bushes beyond.

In her mind, she retraced her steps. That big window must be the parlour, where everyone had gathered for their immunizations. Yes, she could see the stuffed pine marten inside. So the laboratory must be on the other side, across the hallway.

Swallowing her fear, she ran up to the house and pressed herself into the corner where the front wall met the side of the porch. It formed a little blind spot. Nobody who opened the front door would see her there, as the porch wall would hide her.

She crouched down, below the height of the windows, and began to edge along the front wall of the house. By lifting her head ever so slightly, she could peep into the windows as she passed. If anyone was in the room, she could duck back out of sight.

She cautiously peered into the first window. There was the hall with the chequered floor and the grandfather clock. She was going the right way.

She shuffled along further, trying not to make too much noise. A crow flew up from the bushes, squawking, and she stood like a statue until the sounds had died away. The next window had to be the laboratory. She raised her head to look in.

All she saw was heavy cloth. The curtains were drawn. Grinding her teeth in frustration, she shuffled to the next window along. That was blocked by a curtain too.

Stupid of me! Why'd I think this was going to be easy?

She'd reached the corner of the house. Maybe the curtains on the side window would be open? She craned her head round to see. Lizzie breathed in sharply as she saw a room she recognized.

Doctor Gladwell's laboratory was the same room from her vision. There were cloudy flasks full of liquid, a sink, and a pair of bloodstained gloves. Lizzie couldn't see all the way in from here, but she thought she could make out the end of the metal table.

She peered in through the muck on the window, leaning closer for a better view. There were two bare, white feet on the metal table. And the body they belonged to was definitely dead. Was it Becky's father or not? Lizzie couldn't quite see. She tried to squeeze up even closer.

She never heard the crunch of footsteps on gravel, coming up behind her. Someone grabbed her roughly by the arm. Lizzie yelped in fear and looked up into the pop-eyed, grotesquely ugly face of Mrs Crowe.

'You're hurting me! Get off!' Lizzie cried as the old woman's fingers gripped her arm.

'What are you doing here?' the crone demanded with a spray of spittle. 'What did you see?'

'I saw enough!' Lizzie tried to tug herself free, but the old woman's fingers were like a harpy's claws.

'You shouldn't go sticking your nose in where it doesn't belong. There's plenty goes on in the world that a little chit of a girl like you can't hope to understand.'

You can't scare me, Lizzie thought.

'You're wrong,' she told Mrs Crowe. 'I do know what you're up to. You're a witch!'

Mrs Crowe laughed. It was an ugly wet sound, like a cat sicking up a hairball. 'I've been called worse.'

'What's in them jars, eh? Potions? And I know about your needles too. You might have fooled the doctor, but you can't fool me.'

The old woman's hand swept back, ready to slap Lizzie around the face. Lizzie flinched in anticipation. But the blow never came. Mrs Crowe pulled her close, and growled, 'You run along back home, now, if you know what's good for you.'

Lizzie screwed up her face in disgust. Revulsion gave her strength, and in one swift move she wrenched her arm out of Mrs Crowe's grip and shoved her, sending her staggering back into the rhododendrons. Angry yells rang in her ears as she ran for the door: 'Stay back! Get out of there!'

Lizzie sprinted through the open front door and skidded to a halt on the chequered tiles of the hall. *I have to warn Doctor Gladwell,* she thought. *His housekeeper's a witch, and he doesn't even suspect. She's cooking up spells under his roof, using bits of dead bodies.*

'Doctor?' she shouted. 'Doctor, where are you?'

There was a sound of a door closing, then unhurried footsteps descending the stairs. Doctor Gladwell emerged into the hallway, his usual kindly smile lighting up his face. 'I say. It's young Lizzie, isn't it? Whatever can be the matter?'

'It's Mrs Crowe,' Lizzie blurted out. 'She's a witch!'

'Oh dear. Have the village children been telling stories again?'

'I was outside the house, and she grabbed me—'

The doctor tutted and shook his head. 'I'll have to have words. She can be fearsome, but that's no reason to call an old lady cruel names.'

'I looked in the window. There was a dead body on the table!'

The doctor's smile never faltered. 'Ah. Now I see. I'm afraid that's common practice, Lizzie. I'm sorry if you got a nasty shock, but I did tell you to stay away from the laboratory.'

'Common practice?' Lizzie was dumbfounded.

'Doctors have to dissect cadavers, my dear. It's part of our medical training. You can't learn about the human body from books alone, you know.' He put his hands behind his back and strode across the hall until he was standing in front of the door to the laboratory. 'It's not nice, especially not to a young girl, but it's a crucial part of scientific progress.'

'You mean *you* cut up the bodies?'

'Naturally. So do doctors across London. Across the country. Hundreds of them.'

He stopped, as if he realized he'd said too much.

Lizzie looked into his grey eyes. The atmosphere in the room changed. The doctor knew what she was going to ask next, and Lizzie knew that he knew. A sinister feeling crept over her.

'So … if doctors are cutting up bodies all over the country … then where do all the bodies come from?'

'They are the bodies of executed prisoners,' he said, a little too smoothly. 'Now, I'd like to return to my work, if you please.'

'All of them?'

The doctor snapped, 'Yes, all of them!' The mask of kindly good humour was gone. He glared at her as if he wanted to crush her to a pulp. Now his eyes were colder than the glass eyes of his stuffed birds of prey.

'Show me the body you've got in your lab right now,' Lizzie demanded.

'Absolutely not.'

She took a step forward. 'Show me!'

'It's not a suitable sight for young eyes.'

As he blustered, Lizzie charged at the door. She shouldered the doctor aside, grabbed the handle, twisted it and shoved.

The door opened onto the laboratory. The stench hit her, the smell she'd noticed before. It definitely wasn't carbolic. *It's embalming fluid,* she thought. *The smell of dead bodies in an undertaker's parlour.*

The door opened wider, revealing Doctor Gladwell's secret. Finally, Lizzie saw the true horror in the room, and in that moment everything that had happened up to that point made shocking sense. Her stomach heaved.

What she saw on the table would haunt her imagination for months to come…

CHAPTER 17

Becky's father, Jacob Hayward, lay on the examining table with only a white cloth covering him below the waist. He had been laid out like a butchered hog. There was a fresh, open incision in his stomach, exposing his innards.

Lizzie couldn't take her eyes away from it. She had never seen what was inside a human body before.

After the shock of the sight came the horror of understanding. She should have seen it before, back when the graverobbers were dumping Jacob Hayward's clothes into the canal. They were getting rid of the evidence.

They dug him up. No wonder he's not at peace.

Doctor Gladwell had clearly been cutting up dead bodies for many years. The jars on the shelves didn't contain witches' potions, as Lizzie had guessed. What was inside was even worse. They were pickled human organs. She saw kidneys, a wrinkled lung, what looked like a brain. The jars' contents were cloudy and decomposed, and the smell nearly made her retch.

'I told you not to look,' said Doctor Gladwell from behind her. 'Now, aren't you sorry you did?'

'Those graverobbers weren't after jewels and gold at all,' Lizzie said in a hollow voice. 'It was the bodies they wanted. Bodies for you to cut up on your slab!' She rounded on him. 'That was your scheme, wasn't it? You knew when a fresh body was going into the ground, because you're the doctor. People trusted you. So you sent those two thugs out to dig the bodies up and bring them here.'

'You're right,' he said. 'Not that it matters, because nobody will believe you.'

'It's disgusting! That man there isn't one of your experiments. He's my friend's father. She loved him!'

'What would you rather?' the doctor said, trying – and failing – to sound friendly again. 'That the dead should merely rot away, giving no help to anyone? The cadavers I dissect are all making priceless contributions to science. Some part of them lives on, in the form of knowledge! Isn't that better than just feeding the worms in some cemetery somewhere?'

'You had no right,' Lizzie said fiercely. 'The dead deserve to be left in peace.'

The doctor smiled a tight, smug little smile that made Lizzie furious. He slapped Jacob Hayward's cold arm. 'Don't be so sentimental. This is only flesh. There's nothing of the person left.'

'You're wrong,' Lizzie said with total certainty.

He waved a hand dismissively. 'Superstitious nonsense.' He rummaged among the instruments, as if he had work to be getting on with and Lizzie was nothing but an annoying distraction.

She couldn't believe how stubborn and arrogant he was. 'What about the law? Bodysnatching ain't legal. A clever man like you ought to know that. It's a crime. A disgusting crime at that.'

'Men of science are above the laws of common men,' he said, without looking up. The metal tools rattled as he continued searching for something.

Lizzie wanted to wipe that smug smile off his

face. 'Your two mates ain't above the law, I'll tell you that much,' she raged. 'They got carted off by the coppers last night.'

'Indeed?' the doctor said with maddening calm.

'That's right. We caught them. So you won't be getting any more bodies, will you?'

The doctor had found what he was looking for – a razor-sharp scalpel. He raised it up in front of his face. He was no longer smiling. His eyes swivelled around to fix their cold glare on Lizzie.

'No more bodies? Oh, I wouldn't say *that*.'

His meaning was all too clear. Lizzie backed away from him. 'No,' she stammered. 'No. Don't hurt me.'

'Stupid child. You rob me of my cadavers; why shouldn't I turn you into one? It's what you deserve.' With his free hand, he reached for the door handle. He pushed it shut, then twisted the key in the lock and pulled it out. 'There. Now we won't be disturbed.'

'Get away from me!'

He advanced on her. 'Don't be scared. It's just like getting an injection. It only hurts for a second – then it's all over.' The scalpel slashed through the air, not close enough to cut her … not yet. He was trying to scare her, Lizzie knew. And it was working.

She had to fight. Desperately, she snatched a jar from the shelf and flung it. He dodged out of the way and the jar exploded on the floor behind him, spilling its unspeakable contents like slops across the tiles. The stench of preserving fluid was suddenly thick and choking.

'Keep still!' He jabbed at Lizzie, sending her scurrying backwards, pressing her back against the wall. He bared his teeth and changed his grip, holding the scalpel like a dagger in his balled fist, then stabbing downwards with it.

It caught the fabric of her dress and ripped it. Lizzie felt a wet, stinging sensation. He'd cut her, but not deep, thank God…

As he brought the scalpel down again, she caught his wrist and struggled. He grunted as he pushed the blade down towards her neck. It was her strength against his, and he was winning. The shining blade gradually descended.

'I will not let … a circus urchin … get in the way of scientific progress!' he grated. The blade was only an inch away from her throat now. Lizzie fought for her life, drawing on every scrap of strength she had left.

The door crashed open. Mrs Crowe burst in, a bunch

of keys in her hand. The doctor glanced up, taken by surprise. In that moment, his grip relaxed.

Lizzie seized her chance. She flung him back with a wild yell, sending him crashing into the shelves. Jars fell off and smashed on the floor.

'I could turn a blind eye to the graverobbing,' Mrs Crowe shouted, pointing an accusing finger at the struggling doctor, 'but I won't let you cut that girl's throat! You stay away from her, Doctor Gladwell!'

'Shut up, you ignorant old fool,' he spat. 'I should have disposed of you long ago.'

'Run, girl,' Mrs Crowe said, holding the door open. 'You run and tell the police everything this man's done.'

'He'll kill you!' Lizzie yelled.

'I'm old. I've had my time. Go!'

Lizzie made a move for the door, but the doctor stepped into her path. 'Looks like I'm going to need a new housekeeper. That's a shame. Seeing as there's going to be a lot of mess to clean up.'

He drew back his arm for the killing blow.

A black shape, growling like a demon unleashed from the underworld, came bounding through the open door on four paws. It launched itself at the doctor and knocked him sprawling. Doctor Gladwell screamed and thrashed about, while the monstrous beast tore and tugged at his clothes.

'Shadow!' Lizzie shouted in delight.

The dog closed his jaws on the doctor's throat, waiting for the command to finish him off. His big brown eyes looked up at Lizzie, full of loyal devotion. The doctor could only squeal and make a bubbling noise of total fear.

'Hold him,' Lizzie ordered. 'Good boy.'

Malachy and Hari came charging into the room, shouting Shadow's name. 'Here he is!' yelled Malachy. 'Lizzie? Oh God, you're hurt.'

'It ain't deep,' Lizzie said. 'I'm fine. Shadow saved me. That doctor wanted to slice me up.'

'The *doctor* was behind all this?' Hari looked at the dead body on the table and the scalpel in the doctor's hand, and nodded. 'Of course. I should have worked it out long ago.'

'I don't think you'll be needing *this* any more.' Lizzie snatched the scalpel out of the doctor's hand.

'Call your dog off!' the doctor shrieked. 'I'm bleeding. I'll take you to court. I'll have this dog destroyed!'

Lizzie looked down at him in contempt. 'You'll be going to court all right. But Shadow won't be the one who gets his lights put out.'

'I'm sorry, girl,' Mrs Crowe said, hanging her head. 'I should never have let any of this happen. I knew it was wrong, but I didn't dare speak up.'

'You saved my life,' Lizzie said. 'I owe you for that.'

'We need to tie this bloke up,' Malachy said, 'before Shadow chews his head off.'

Lizzie rummaged around in the cabinets and found a roll of bandage. While she and Malachy tied the doctor hand and foot, Hari sprinted off to fetch the police. Mrs Crowe silently left the room.

'Where are you going?' Malachy shouted after her.

'I'm making some tea,' she replied. 'Don't worry, boy. I won't run off. I wouldn't get far, anyway, not at my age.'

Lizzie thought of JoJo and his delirious raving about needles. She sprang to her feet. 'JoJo! I almost forgot about him. He's still in this house!'

She raced up the stairs, leaving Malachy and Shadow to guard the fallen doctor. JoJo's door was slightly open. She barged her way in and stood staring in horror at what she saw.

At first she thought JoJo was dead. His face was a pitted mess, his lips dry and cracked. But when he saw her, they drew back in a slow, painful smile. 'Lizzie? Is that you?'

'JoJo, you're alive!' She ran and hugged him, despite the dreadful smell coming from his bedsheets. 'Just hang on a bit longer. The police are coming. We're going to get you out of here.'

'The doctor … he's up to no good. Don't trust him.' JoJo tried to sit up and fell back, coughing.

'He ain't a problem any more. We stopped him.'

JoJo angled his head towards the trolley laden with medical implements. 'He never meant to cure me at all. He's been doing experiments on me.'

'*Experiments?*'

'Injecting me with … what did he call them? Bacteria. And other things. Then taking my blood to look at under his microscope.'

Lizzie could see the clown was getting worse, not better. 'We'll take you back to the circus and we'll take care of you ourselves. Don't die, OK? Please!'

JoJo closed his eyes. 'I begged him not to do it. "Please let me live," I said. "All I want to do is make people laugh again." But he said I was useless. "What's more pathetic than a clown?" he said to me. "You'll be more use as a corpse."'

More use as a corpse. Lizzie knew exactly what that meant. The doctor was planning to cut JoJo up after he died. With tears in her eyes, she held the clown's hand and made a promise. Even if JoJo didn't make it, she'd see him buried decently. No doctor would get his hands on her friend's body.

She was still sitting there when the police arrived. The doctor protested his innocence, but the constable cut him short. 'I knew Jacob Hayward,' he said, 'and that's him, right there on that filthy slab, when he ought to be resting in his grave. He was a better man than you. You're no doctor, Gladwell. You're a butcher.'

'What I did, I did for science,' the doctor snarled.

'Science? Was it the Royal Society you had your eye on, eh? Some great medical prize? Well, I'll tell you one thing. You're going to be famous after today. Your phizog's going to be in the papers from here to John o' Groats.' The constable drained his tea. 'Thanks for the brew, Mrs Crowe, but I'm afraid I'm going to have to ask you to come with us, now.'

Mrs Crowe held out her hands for the handcuffs

and sighed. 'Do your duty, Constable.'

Outside the house, Lizzie hugged Hari and Malachy and gave Shadow a grateful stroke. 'I nearly got my throat cut in there,' she said with a shiver. 'Thanks for coming after me.'

'I should have come with you in the first place, Lizzie,' Malachy said, looking embarrassed. 'Stupid of me to think I knew better than you did! Your visions have never been wrong before. They don't call you the Magnificent Lizzie Brown for nothing!'

CHAPTER 18

That night, the show tent was packed. An electric feeling of excitement crackled in the air, and the wide-eyed audience burst into wild applause the moment they saw Fitzy appear, before he could even say a word.

He jumped back, faking surprise, then gave them a huge grin and raised his arms. 'Welcome, one and all, to the hardest working circus on the planet!' the ringmaster boomed.

Lizzie watched from behind the curtain, her heart hammering. All the wild adventure of the last few days had to be put aside now. She had to focus on her performance. Doubts were chasing their tails in her mind.

We've hardly rehearsed. The comedy might not work. What if Victoria spooks again?

Fitzy introduced the Boissets to another storm of applause. Lizzie looked on open-mouthed as Dru, Collette and their family put on one of the best performances she'd ever seen. The more the audience cheered, the more their confidence seemed to grow. Dru couldn't put a foot wrong even if he'd tried.

'That's more like it,' Malachy said. 'The Boissets are back on form.'

Hari nodded. 'My animals seem calmer too. It could just be the change in the weather, I suppose. But I think they're happier because we're happier.'

'The dead are at peace, so the jinx is broken,' Erin said.

'If there ever *was* a jinx.' Lizzie still wasn't willing to open the door more than a crack where superstition was concerned. Even, she told herself, if she *had* spoken to ghosts.

Erin gave Lizzie a tolerant look and a smile that said *one day, you'll understand.*

The next few acts seemed to rush past in a blur. Clowns, acrobats and performing animals all played their parts as if they had been blessed. That just made

Lizzie more nervous. What if she was going to be the one to mess it all up? She chewed on her fingernail.

Nora slapped her wrist lightly. 'Stop it.'

'I can't help it. I haven't got butterflies in my tummy, I've got ruddy elephants.'

'You'll be fine.'

'Elephants with hobnail boots on.'

Hari whispered, 'Victoria's not nervous. So why should you be?'

Lizzie stared. The midnight-black horse was standing perfectly still, the blinkers she wore screening her from any distraction.

'Trust the horses,' Hari said. 'And trust yourself.'

Fitzy's voice boomed out over the applause. 'And now, ladies and gents, for the act you've all been waiting for. You've read about them in the papers, you've seen their picture on the posters, but nothing can prepare you for the reality! Here they are, fresh from their triumphant tour of Kensal Green Cemetery…'

The crowd roared with laughter.

'…the Amazing Sullivan Twins!'

This one's for you, JoJo, Lizzie thought.

Lizzie and Nora rode out into the light. They circled the tent, waving at the audience and smiling, while the band played an opening fanfare. Then there was a roll on the drums. The audience fell silent. All eyes were on Lizzie as she lifted herself up to stand on Albert's back. She reached out her arms to balance, then deliberately rolled her eyes back, waggled her arms and fell straight down on her bottom. A trombone made a loud *parp*.

Delighted laughter roared from the stalls. Nora put her hands on her hips in mock impatience, and to the accompaniment of a second drum-roll, stood upright – and then balanced on one leg, lifting her toe to touch her outstretched fingers. The trumpets blared *ta-daaaaa!*

It was the simplest stunt in Nora's repertoire, and yet the audience applauded like never before. Nora and Lizzie exchanged a private look, and Lizzie knew they were both thinking the same thing: *This is going to work.* Best of all, Victoria was still calm and docile, happy in her blinkers.

The rest of the act went from strength to strength. Lizzie fumbled juggling clubs, but Nora caught them. Lizzie's pirouette ended with her sprawled across Albert's back like a flopping fish, while Nora's drew gasps of amazement. By the time Lizzie deliberately botched her leap from Albert's back and fell into

Dru's waiting arms, she was almost sorry to have to leave the ring.

A girl could get used to this, she thought, as Dru carried her triumphantly away from the applause, through the curtain and into the crowd of her waiting friends.

'Do you want to count it again, Pop?' Malachy asked Fitzy. They were sitting in their caravan, sorting an immense pile of notes and coins into neat order.

'I don't think so, son. Three times is enough.'

'It's our best night this year,' Malachy told Lizzie. 'This isn't just ticket sales. They were throwing money into the ring at the end! Can you believe it?'

'It's good luck to throw coins into a circus ring,' Fitzy said, very seriously. Then he winked. 'Good luck for me, at least.'

Lizzie felt an uncomfortable prickle at the back of her neck, as if she were being watched. She turned to see the dark figures of Calculating Crake and Persuading Harry advancing slowly on the caravan. Harry was wearing his brass knuckles, and it looked like he was eager to use them.

'Mr Fitzgerald...' she warned.

'Ah, gentlemen!' Fitzy noticed them and came down the caravan steps. 'How wonderful to see you. What an interesting aroma. Is that a new cologne, perhaps? Oh, never mind, I see it's something you've stepped in. That's one of the problems with owning elephants, I find.'

'Time's up, Fitzgerald,' said Crake. 'We've been more than generous.'

'Generous,' echoed Harry.

'And since the debt ain't been settled, we'll just have to take payment in kind. Starting with those two horses.'

Fitzy snapped his fingers. 'I knew there was something I meant to do. Malachy!'

'What's this?' Crake said, deeply suspicious.

Malachy came out with an envelope stuffed with notes. He handed it to Crake, who swiftly counted it and passed it to Harry for safekeeping.

'It's all the money we owe you, to the penny,' Fitzy said. 'I suggest you take it.'

Crake looked around at the brightly coloured caravans and tents, then shrugged and turned to leave. 'Till next time, Fitz.'

'Toodle-oo, cheerio, go jump in front of a train,' Fitzy muttered through his teeth, still grinning. He didn't take his eyes off the money-lenders until they were safely off the site. Then a strange expression came over him. His eyes gleamed. 'Trains. Now there's an idea.' He began to stride through the site towards the tea tent. 'A circus train! If we keep packing the house like we did tonight, we could afford one!'

Malachy started off after him. 'Dad, no!'

'Just think. No more trudging down endless country roads. No more rain and wind. The comfort of a dining car!'

'Dad, how many times? You have to be practical...'

Their voices dwindled into the distance.

Not long after, Lizzie let herself into JoJo's caravan. She silently moved to stand at the clown's bedside. There were flowers on a table next to him. She looked down at his peaceful face. She thought his spots were looking better.

His eyes flickered open. 'Wotcher, Lizzie.'

'How are you feeling, mate?' She passed him a cup of water.

'About a million times better, thanks.' He slurped

it, gargled, swallowed and winked. 'Ma Sullivan and Anita have been fussing over me like a pair of hens. How did your act go?'

She sat down on the bed. 'They liked us. I did better as a clown than a serious performer.'

'Right. I'd better hurry up and get this pox beat. I reckon someone's after my job.'

'Oh, don't you worry,' she said with a laugh. 'As soon as Erin's better, I'm back to fortune-telling full time!'

The next morning, the Penny Gaff Gang gathered at the gates of Kensal Green Cemetery to meet Becky. Hari led Shadow on a leash.

When Becky arrived, she was walking alongside a funeral carriage. The black coffin it bore was smart and new, the best Lizzie's money could buy.

'Thank you,' Becky whispered as Lizzie went to walk by her side. 'For everything.'

While the friends stood and watched, Jacob Hayward was laid to rest once more, in a grave he would never again be snatched from. Instead of the simple wooden cross, a proud headstone now stood. The officiating priest spoke kindly of the power of love to outlast death, and the certainty of reunion in the hereafter.

All through the service, Lizzie turned the horse brass over and over in her pocket. She didn't hear so much as a whisper from beyond. Becky's father was indeed at rest.

'Ashes to ashes,' the priest intoned, 'and dust to dust.'

'Just a moment,' Lizzie said. While the others looked on in surprise, she quickly slipped the horse brass on top of the coffin lid. Becky smiled in grateful understanding – the brass she'd given her father had been thrown into the canal. Now he had a replacement.

Once the funeral was over and all the tears had been wiped away, the friends gathered at the cemetery gates for a final goodbye. Becky hugged Lizzie so tight she thought a rib might crack.

'I'll miss you,' Becky whispered.

Lizzie thought of the chickens running wild in the farmyard and all the hard jobs that would need to be done on the farm. She saw Becky alone and weary, sitting at a table too big for just one person, with nobody to care for, or to care for her.

'You could come with us,' she said. 'Join the circus. You're good with animals. Hari could use a bit more help, couldn't you, Hari?'

'Always!' Hari said. 'If you can handle a cow, I'm sure you can handle an elephant.'

Becky shook her head. 'It's lovely of you. But I'm a farmer, and this is my home. My pa fought to keep it. I can't just walk away.'

'Well, then,' Hari said, 'maybe one of us should stay here with you.'

Becky looked confused.

Hari handed her Shadow's leash. The dog lay down at Becky's feet, as if to protect her from anyone who might wish her harm.

'He took to you from the start,' Hari said. 'So he should be yours. A guardian and a companion.'

Becky hugged the dog, who licked her face. 'It's wonderful … I don't know what to say!'

'How about "see you next year"?' Lizzie said with a smile.

'That'll do. When you're back in Kensal Green, come and see us. You know where to find me!' Becky whistled and the dog stood up. 'Come on, boy. We're going home.'

The Penny Gaff Gang waved their farewells and began the long walk back to the circus tents.

'I wonder what it's like,' Malachy wondered aloud. 'Living in one place, the *same* place, all the time.'

'I can't imagine it,' said Nora.

'Nor me,' said Erin.

Dru made a face. 'I think, if I were not always on the road, I would feel dead inside.'

'What about you, Lizzie?' Hari said. 'You're the only one of us who's known it both ways. Do you miss living in a fixed place?'

Lizzie looked at the hedgerows they were walking past. Dandelion seeds were blowing in the wind, the air carrying them far and free above all boundaries, like the roaming thoughts of a storyteller, or the wild dreams of a girl with her whole life still to live.

'No. My home is always on the move now,' she smiled. 'And that's just how I like it.'

Read on for a sneak peek of the next
Lizzie Brown adventure, **THE GHOST SHIP**…

CHAPTER 1

Fitzy, who was both owner and ringmaster of the circus that bore his name, stood alone in the sawdust ring and lifted his gigantic hat to the audience.

'Ladies and gentlemen of Oxford – dear friends all! – it has been a pleasure to entertain you for so many nights. But alas, all good things must come to an end.'

The audience sighed an *awwww*, but Fitzy dismissed it. 'No tears, I beg you. I ask only this: For one final time, please show your appreciation for the stars of our show, every one of them!' He brandished his cane. 'Maestro, please!'

As the band struck up with a rum-tum-tiddly

fanfare, the various acts came prancing back into the ring. The coloured lights brightened, the audience cheered and clapped, and Fitzy stood among it all beaming like a lighthouse.

Nobody in the audience could see the two children who hid behind the beaded curtain, waving and grinning to their performer friends as they headed back out. One was Lizzie Brown, the circus's resident fortune teller, who – unlike most side-show psychics – genuinely had the ability to see into the future. The other was Fitzy's son Malachy, whose club foot couldn't slow down his razor-sharp mind.

'The Amazing Sullivan Sisters!' Fitzy announced.

Lizzie's best friends, the twins Erin and Nora, trotted past her on the backs of their flawless black horses. Both girls had long red hair, bound up in long plaits and fastened with silver brooches, and wore ballet dresses specially designed to be worn in the saddle.

Nora gave Lizzie a wave and wink. As they entered the ring, they stood up in their saddles, then tumbled over to stand on their hands. Lizzie watched, holding her breath with excitement, while the two girls entranced the audience once again.

Beside her, Malachy laughed. 'It's the same show

they do every night. Aren't you tired of watching yet?'

'Never,' Lizzie said.

How could she ever get tired of this? She was still new to the circus, true, but she knew the wonder of it all would never fade, no matter how much hard work needed to be done or how many early starts had to be endured. This brightly coloured world, always on the move, was where she belonged.

'Those merry masters of mayhem, the clowns!'

The clowns came charging past her in answer to Fitzy's call, but the moment they burst into the ring, they fell over, tumbling head-over-heels or slamming into one another. The audience roared with laughter. Lizzie smiled to see her friend JoJo chucking buckets of confetti about. Not long ago, he had been gravely ill with smallpox. Lizzie was happy to see that he was back to his old self.

'Good crowd tonight,' Malachy said, flipping a shiny shilling in his hand and catching it. 'Best pitch in a long time, this is.'

'I bet your dad's pleased.'

'Too right. After Kensal Green, this is just what he needed. He looks ten years younger, doesn't he?'

Lizzie shuddered at the memory of Kensal Green. Setting up the circus so close to London's biggest cemetery hadn't worked out very well. All the animals had been skittish and the crowds slow in coming. Then Erin had been hurt too badly to perform, which meant no star turn and angry customers demanding refunds. And on top of all that, there had been the strange affair of the Devil's Hound… Everything had worked out in the end, thanks to the Penny Gaff Gang, but it had nearly bankrupted Fitzy.

'Thank heaven nothing's gone wrong here in Oxford,' she muttered. 'Not so far, anyway.'

She didn't tell Malachy, but that was her other reason for watching the show every night. It was becoming almost superstitious. She didn't dare miss it, in case something bad happened.

'The Astonishing Boissets!' Fitzy announced, hurling his cane up into the air.

The lights swivelled to reveal the high-wire. The audience gasped as the family of French daredevils came trooping out to take their bows. The wire trembled under their weight. Dru Boisset was in the centre – dark-haired, handsome and all of fourteen years old.

Lizzie's knuckle went to her mouth. No matter how many times she saw their act, her nerves were always in knots. Even the presence of the safety net didn't help.

Malachy grinned. 'Do you think he can see you from up there?'

'Eh?' Lizzie glared at him.

'Does he know you watch him every night? Don't worry. I won't tell. But we both know why you're really here, Liz.'

'You cheeky little beggar!' Lizzie cried, storming towards him with her fist raised.

Malachy cringed away, laughing.

'Dru's just a friend and you know it,' Lizzie insisted. 'But I've seen you making puppy eyes at the twins!' *Sooner or later*, she thought, *I'll figure out which of the twins Mal has a crush on.*

'Whatever you say, mate.'

'One of these days I'll give you a fat lip,' Lizzie grumbled. She wasn't really angry, and Malachy was hardly the only one of her friends who teased her about Dru. But if she didn't lash out like this, they might realise that the sight of the boy really did make her insides go all fluttery.

Fitzy introduced the tumbling acrobats, the boys of the Sullivan family riding their ponies, and lastly the stately elephants led by Hari, the Indian boy who was another of Lizzie's close friends. She was determined not to stare at Dru now, just to show Malachy, so she let her gaze rove over the audience instead.

They really were a well-to-do lot, this Oxford crowd. Men with top hats like a row of chimney pots, ladies with skin as pale as bone china, children in sailor suits and knickerbockers bouncing up and down in their seats… Lizzie guessed not one of those rosy-faced kids knew what it was like to go without a single meal, let alone face starvation.

She would have been jealous of children like that, back in the days when she lived in the London slum of Rat's Castle. They had lollipops and toys, while she had had to struggle for a crust of bread. But her fortune telling had taught her some surprising lessons. Even the richest of families could have terrible secrets, she now knew, and a pampered childhood didn't always mean happiness.

'Thank you once again, ladies and gentlemen, and goodnight!'

As Fitzy bowed, turned and bowed again, Lizzie noticed something strange in the front row. In the row of top hats, one of the heads was covered in bandages.

No, not bandages – a turban!

She could see the gentleman clearly now. 'Strewth,'

she said, impressed. He was strikingly handsome, with dark skin like Hari's and elegantly cut clothes. Not shy of a bob or two, then. And were those jewelled rings on his fingers?

The English people beside him were clapping politely, but the stylish gentleman was showing no such restraint. 'Bravo!' he shouted, applauding wildly. 'Encore!'

Lizzie grinned to see an adult enjoying himself so much. Usually, only children would react with this kind of wild excitement. Either this man didn't realise it wasn't quite proper to go overboard like this, or he didn't care. Nobody was shushing him, at any rate. Maybe they didn't dare to.

The lady sitting next to him was smiling and looking at him fondly. Was she his wife? She was blonde and beautiful, like a painting from the top of a tin of chocolates. Lizzie thought she must have seen her somewhere before, in the papers, maybe. She looked like a society lady, or perhaps an actress or a foreign princess. She held a broad fan with peacock feathers, slowly fanning herself, and Lizzie was reminded of the way a cat's tail will sometimes lash slowly, when it's sitting and thinking.

Then the feeling was upon her, gripping her whole body as suddenly as a sneeze and every bit as impossible to control. Lizzie let out a tiny gasp, and then stood stock still as pictures began to appear in her mind.

I'm having one of me visions! she thought, fearful and excited at once. Most of the time, her visions appeared when she was doing readings for people, but they sometimes struck out of the blue, just like this one. They were much stronger than the others, and they always warned of trouble to come…

To find out what happens next, read

THE GHOST SHIP

Don't miss the first book in

THE MAGNIFICENT LIZZIE BROWN

series

Roll up, roll up! A hair-raising adventure is about to unfold!

Join Lizzie Brown, the fortuneteller's assistant, and her gang of circus friends, as they try to uncover the identity of the mysterious phantom.

In Victorian London, a masked figure has been thieving from houses and evading the police. When Lizzie Brown has a psychic vision about the burglar, she knows she has to act. But this phantom is proving to be more dangerous than a tightrope without a safety net…

For more exciting books from brilliant authors, follow the fox!

www.curious-fox.com